Also by Maudie Smith

Opal Moonbaby
About Zooming Time, Opal Moonbaby!

OPAL MOONBABY
FOREVER

OPAL MOONBABY FOREVER

Maudie Smith

Illustrated by Dave Shepherd

Orion
Children's Books

First published in Great Britain in 2014
by Orion Children's Books
a division of the Orion Publishing Group Ltd
Orion House
5 Upper St Martin's Lane
London WC2H 9EA
A Hachette UK Company

1 3 5 7 9 10 8 6 4 2

A catalogue record for this book is available from the British Library.

ISBN 978 1 4440 0480 9

Printed in Great Britain by Clays Ltd, St Ives plc

The Orion Publishing Group's policy is to use papers that are natural,
renewable and recyclable products made from wood grown in sustainable
forests. The logging and manufacturing processes are expected to conform
to the environmental regulations of the country of origin.

www.orionbooks.co.uk

For Jo

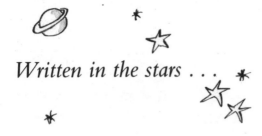

Written in the stars . . .

Have you ever had a proper look at the night sky? Stand outside on a cloudless night, far away from the city, well away from every single street light, and you might just see it.

Billions of stars, twinkling away. The trickiest dot-to-dot the world has ever known.

And those are the stars of just one galaxy. What if we could look further still? How many more millions of stars and planets we would see! Planets that humans have never named. Planets that humans have never even set eyes on.

Planets like Carnelia.

If you could see all the way to Carnelia, you would see the Carnelians themselves, an alien race going about their daily business as if Earth, and you, didn't even exist.

1

There is one man up there, though, who knows all about Earth and Earth dwellers. He wears a crown and sits in a great empty hall, drumming long fingers on the arm of his high-backed chair.

He is alone apart from a small bat-like creature, no bigger than a folded handkerchief, which from time to time sticks its head out of the man's breast pocket and looks around. Like its owner, it seems to be waiting for something.

Not something. Some*one*.

Someone who has been away from Carnelia for a long time.

The creature gazes at its master. A question is clear in its golden-eagle eyes.

The Carnelian Coronet-holder – for that is who the man is – strokes his mingle's crested head with one thumb. His bright blue eyes glitter with his answer.

'Yes, she will soon be finished with Earth. Opal Moonbaby will soon be home.'

Summer Schedule of Stuff To Do

1. Go to the Skateboard Bowl Fun Fete

Martha stopped writing for a moment, hoisted herself onto the kitchen counter and looked down at the park.

The Skateboard Bowl Fun Fete was happening today, in one hour to be precise. People were already setting up their stalls. There was a bouncy castle being inflated, and the man with the Bucking Bronco had arrived. The Bucking Bronco was going to be the highlight of the afternoon. It was a machine that looked a bit like a bull. You were supposed to sit on it while it shook and jerked

about, and try not to get thrown off. Martha wanted to go straight down and see it but she had promised herself she would finish the schedule first. Anyway, the next part was easy. She had it all planned out.

2. Go to the end of the road and back
3. Play Hide and Seek
4. Visit mini-market
5. Look at ads on bus shelter
6. Spy on people in office block
7. Chase bikes
8. Hang out in play-pipe

Those were the things they had done last summer. If they did them all again, Martha thought, then this summer would be just as brilliant as that one had been. The activities didn't look like much on paper – most people would think they were pretty boring things to do – but then most people hadn't tried doing them with an alien. Most people didn't have an alien for a best friend. Not like Martha.

Like other young Carnelians before her, Opal had been sent on a mission to Earth and given tasks to prove her worth. Once she had completed the tasks she would get her Carnelian Independence Award. Making a human friend had been one of Opal's tasks. Martha hadn't wanted to be friends at first, but that was then. Now they were the best friends in the world. Nothing could keep them apart.

9. Try out new skateboard bowl - if it's finished in time

Martha checked the calendar she was using to lean on. She had put a tiny dot against the twenty-sixth of August. That was the date she never wanted to come. But it was still three whole weeks away. The skateboard bowl was sure to be ready before that. There would be plenty of time to do all the other things on her list too. Three weeks was ages and ages.

She clicked the end of her pen against her teeth and gazed out of the window.

Not that the skateboard bowl looked anywhere near ready at the moment. There wasn't much to see where the old bandstand had been demolished to make way for it. Just a heap of earth and a muddy hole that looked like a messy dinosaur footprint. The heap had been surrounded by orange netting and KEEP OFF signs for months. Now someone had strung red and blue bunting all over it, ready for the Fun Fete. If the Fete raised enough money, the workmen would come back and finish the bowl and they would be able to skateboard in it before the summer was over. Before number 10 had to happen.

Martha chewed the pen. She knew exactly what Number 10 was but she couldn't bring herself to write it down. It had to go on the list because it had to be done, but if she could have one wish in the world, just one, it was that the time for Number 10 would never come. She could hardly believe it would. Not today. Not when the sun was shining and there was so much exciting stuff going on. In any case, there was no point thinking about sad things when you were having so much fun you could practically burst.

She'd never seen the park so busy. Everything in it looked incredibly inviting but Martha was saving the best, most inviting bit of the view till last. Out of the corner of her eye she caught sight of something bobbing up and down. She thought for a moment someone was kicking a football up in the air. She smiled when she saw what it really was.

It was Opal Moonbaby's head.

Opal was bouncing up and down outside her little purple house. Behind her, the Domestipod glinted in the sunshine. She was jumping so high she could have been on a trampoline, but Opal didn't have a trampoline; she just had an awful lot of bounce. The sight of her made Martha want to bounce up and down too, right where she was, kneeling on the kitchen counter. Opal always had that effect on her.

They had been friends for almost a year now, but she still got that feeling every day. Opal was the sort of person you could never get tired of. Nothing was boring when Opal was around.

As soon as she looked her way, Opal started waving her arms and beckoning to Martha to join her. They were going to get ready for the Fete together. They were going to visit every single stall. They were going to spend the whole day together, just like they always did. Opal looked as if she was impatient to get started.

'I'll be right down,' Martha mouthed. 'Don't move a muscle till I get there.'

A human being would never have been able to see Martha's lips move from that distance, but Opal could. Her eyes were so powerful she could see exactly what Martha was saying. She stopped bouncing and struck a pose, standing as still as a statue, not moving a muscle.

Martha laughed. Trust Opal! She would stay like that now until she reached her. She looked as if she was prepared to stay there forever.

If only.

10.

Martha was about to fill in the last item on the schedule when the flat door flew open and banged against the wall.

'And the man with the biggest biceps in the world eats fifteen eggs every day. I'd be sick if I had to do that. How big are your biceps, exactly?'

Robbie clattered in with two large buckets hooked over his arms. Martha knew he wasn't talking to her.

'Not that big. My biceps would probably look like ants' eggs if I stood next to that guy.' Sam followed Robbie inside, his tracksuit trousers swishing as he walked. He tossed Mum's keys, the ones with the heart-shaped key ring, onto the counter. 'Hiya, Martha. What's up? Not disturbing you, are we?'

'No,' said Martha. ''Course not.' She held the Summer Schedule close to her chest.

'Good. We've just come to find a couple more sponges.'

Robbie held up his buckets. 'Sam's going to let people throw soggy sponges at him. At point-blank range! How slick is that!' *Slick* was Robbie's latest top-favourite word. He always had a favourite word on the go. Until recently, everything had been *random* or *immense*. Now most things were *slick*.

'I'm used to getting wet,' said Sam, flinging open the cupboard under the kitchen sink. 'It's in the day job.'

'*Well* slick!' said Robbie.

Sam smiled up at Martha where she still knelt on the counter. 'This sponge-throwing will be water off a duck's back for me, won't it?'

'Mm,' murmured Martha. She looked away, feeling her cheeks go pink. She hadn't got used to Sam being around so much.

Sam was Martha and Robbie's swimming instructor. He worked at the leisure centre.

At least, he used to be their swimming instructor. He still was their swimming instructor, but now he was Mum's boyfriend too.

Martha had known for a while that Mum had been going on a few dates, but she'd never asked anyone round to the flat before Sam came along. It had been just the three of them for ages, Mum, Martha and Robbie. Martha liked it that way. Now Sam was showing up all the time. He wasn't horrible, not at all, but his presence made Martha feel a bit uncomfortable, the way she felt if she put her t-shirt on back to front and found the label sticking up against her throat. Sam wasn't something she could sort out as easily as a back-to-front t-shirt, though.

Robbie loved it when Sam came round because he played football and Top Trumps with him, but Martha wasn't so sure. Sam had taken them to the zoo in his car once, and that had been fun, but he had a big, loud laugh and he left half-empty coffee mugs in the bathroom. And he quite often sat in her favourite place on the sofa, next to Mum's spot. It didn't have her name on it or anything but Martha didn't like it when she found him sitting there. She usually went and hung out with Opal when Sam came round. Sometimes, when she bent to pick her shoes off the rack in the hall, she caught the sweaty whiff of his trainers sitting alongside Mum's work pumps and she would move the pumps a little further away, to give them some breathing space.

'What are you counting down to, then?' Sam nodded at the calendar. 'Christmas?'

'No,' said Martha. She clambered down from the counter. 'Nothing like that.'

'Quite right, too,' said Sam. 'You've still got nearly the whole holiday. You'll have lots of summer fun yet!' He winked at her and stuck his head in the cupboard.

Martha wondered what Sam knew about how much summer fun she'd have. It was none of his business. If she told him what she was doing he'd probably want to know all about it. He was like that. Anyway, Opal was still stuck like a statue, so she didn't want him slowing her down with his questions now.

'Here we go. Catch!' Sam tossed two sponges backwards and upwards into the air. Robbie ran forward with his buckets held out and managed to catch one of them. The other landed near Martha's feet.

'You'll have to be quicker than that, Martha,' said Robbie.

'She wasn't ready, that's all.' Sam picked up a frying pan from the draining board. 'Hey, how about I rustle up a few pancakes? Your mum's coming in in a minute. She and Alesha have nearly finished setting up their stall. We could all have a snack before the Fete starts.'

'Great idea!' said Robbie.

'Don't make any for me, thanks.' Martha reached past Sam for a margarine tub she had washed and needed for the Fete. 'I've got to get going.'

'OK,' said Sam. 'See you later, Martha.'

'*Vatengpaxxz*, Martha.' Robbie saluted her with his buckets.

Martha hurried out, frowning. *Vatengpaxxz* was a Carnelian word. It was what Opal and her Uncle Bixbite said to each other whenever they parted. Robbie shouldn't be saying it, though, especially not in front of Sam. Sam wouldn't know what he was on about but they still had to be careful. No one apart from Martha and Robbie knew that Opal was an alien from another planet, and if she was finally going to get her Carnelian Independence Award, that was how it had to stay.

She was relieved to hear Robbie change the subject. 'What's the world record for making pancakes, do you think, Sam?' Someone had given him a copy of the *Guinness Book of World Records* for his birthday, and now he was obsessed with records of all kinds.

In the bedroom Martha skirted round the pyramid of burst footballs Robbie had collected from the park. He was adding new balls to it almost every day, hoping to get into the record book himself. If

Martha accidentally trod on one of them the whole lot would fall down, and then she'd be practically swimming in footballs. It had happened to her several times already.

Quickly, without giving herself more time to think, without even looking at the words as she wrote them, she filled in Number 10 at last. Then she shoved the calendar and the Summer Schedule in her drawer, pushing it firmly shut. She wanted to see Opal and be with her, not worry about how she would soon be leaving Archwell and the Earth for good. How she would have to say goodbye to her.

Goodbye forever.

Opal was still in exactly the same position, one hand pointing to the sky, the other outstretched in front of her. She had a smile fixed on her pale face, and her huge, violet eyes didn't blink once as she stared into the distance. She really could have been made of marble, if it wasn't for her silvery-white hair sticking up as always and waving gently in the summer breeze. The rest of her was so still that a bird had landed on her upturned palm and was sunning itself there.

Garnet, Opal's mingle, hadn't noticed the bird. Martha was surprised about that. Garnet may have been a mix of six different animals, but one of those animals was a cat, and like all cats he loved chasing things. Not today. He was curled up on the window

ledge of the Domestipod, fast asleep.

As she approached, the bird tutted at her and flew away. Martha paused to breathe in Opal's special smell. No one else smelt of sparklers and hot chilli peppers. It was a smell that tickled your nose and told you something fun was about to happen.

She touched Opal's raised arm.

'Hello, Best Friend in the Universe,' said Opal, coming back to life instantly. 'What took you so zooming long?' She turned a series of cartwheels, her skinny legs sticking out of her purple shorts like long twigs. 'I've been standing here for monkey's years. That bird would have built its nest on me if it hadn't been about to fly north.'

'South,' said Martha. 'Birds fly south at the end of summer. Sorry I'm late. I got held up. Have you made the sign for Mrs Underedge's stall?'

Their teacher, Mrs Underedge, was going to tell fortunes at the Fete. She would never have agreed to do something like that last summer, but since Opal had arrived in school, Mrs Underedge was a completely different person. As soon as she'd heard about the Fun Fete, she'd said it sounded like 'a lot of lovely high jinks', and offered to be a fortune-teller. Martha and Opal had volunteered to help set up her tent.

'I certainly have made the sign,' said Opal. 'Garnet's been looking after it for me.' She went over to the window ledge where Garnet was lying on a piece of cardboard. His owl eyes were closed and his stoat nose rested on his front paws. Martha lifted him gently so as not to disturb him too much, while Opal pulled the board out from under him.

''Scuse us, lazy Jones,' Opal said to the mingle. Martha put Garnet back down and he curled up again without so much as a *chi-cha!* He was sleeping an awful lot these days, Martha had noticed.

'Is he?' said Opal, reading her thoughts and seeming concerned suddenly. 'Is he sleeping too much, do you think?'

'Probably not,' said Martha. 'He's just like our cats and dogs – they love snoozing in the sun. Why? Are you worried about him?'

But Opal was already holding up her cardboard sign.

'Well? What do you think?'

Martha read the large yellow lettering.

GYPSY ROSE UNDEREDGE
HEAR YOUR FORTUNE!!
SEE INTO YOUR
FANTABULOUS FUTURE!!!!

She nodded. 'It's good. Great!'

'Mrs U will be puffed away, won't she?' Even though Opal had been on Earth for months, she still managed to get her sayings wrong.

'She'll love it,' Martha said. 'I can't imagine Mrs

Underedge telling people's fortunes, though.'

'I can't imagine anyone telling fortunes,' said Opal, 'since it's not even possible. I never heard anything less logical in my life. Logic is king, you know, Martha.'

'Is it?'

Opal said this as if it was a comment she made every day, but Martha had never heard her say it before.

'Oh yes, you'll never get anywhere without logic. That's what Uncle Bixbite says. Still, it's only a game, isn't it? I love games!'

Martha took a closer look at Opal's sign, which smelt very sweet and was attracting butterflies. 'How have you done the letters?'

'With popcorn,' said Opal. 'It was all I had in the house. I stuck it down with honey. Do you want a bit?' She started to prise one of the puffy popcorn kernels off the board.

'How about later?' Martha said hastily. 'After the Fete?'

'Good point,' said Opal. 'We don't want to spoil it, do we?' She ran her hands over the bumpy letters. 'Let's make some popcorn for ourselves. Have we got time?'

Martha shrugged. 'Sam seems to think so. He's up in the flat making pancakes for Mum. Again.' She rolled her eyes. 'He's always cooking things for her.'

'Is he, now?' said Opal, going in through her green

front door. 'Well, you know what they say.'

'What?'

'The way to a woman's heart is through her intestines!'

'That's not it!' Martha laughed as she followed Opal inside. 'It's through her stomach. And anyway, it's a man's heart in the saying, I think, not a woman's.'

'Same difference,' said Opal, pouring popcorn into the scoff-capsule dispenser. 'Still, I suppose I'd better get it right. Uncle Bixbite doesn't like it if I make mistakes.' Instead of switching on the dispenser, she plucked her *Human Handybook* out of her hammock, sat down next to Martha on the purple beanbags and opened it up.

Opal was compiling the *Human Handybook* herself. It was a book of all the information she had gathered about humans and their way of life. She was going to take it back to her planet for the other Carnelians to read.

The flowery notebook Martha had given Opal to put all the information in was almost full now. It reminded Martha that the date of Opal's Final Ascendance was coming up, and she would soon be returning to Carnelia. Not that Martha wanted any reminders; she was trying to keep that date at the very back of her mind.

'The twenty-sixth of Earth's August,' said Opal, tuning into Martha's thoughts. Even the backs of minds weren't out of bounds for Opal. She crossed out *intestines* and wrote *stomach* in over the top. 'Then I'll have my Carnelian Independence Award. I'll be Opal Moonbaby CIA, and it's off back to Carnelia with me for Coronet training.' Martha watched as she drew a little heart and shaded it in.

'Do you have to start training straight away?'

'Pretty much,' said Opal. 'I'll be Carnelian Coronet-holder in a few months.'

'Really? But that's your Uncle Bixbite's job. And aren't you a bit young, to be in charge of an entire planet, I mean?' Martha knew Opal might have to take charge of Carnelia one day, if she got her CIA and passed all her tests, but she hadn't imagined it happening so quickly.

'Uncle Bixie doesn't think I'm too young. He can't wait for me to overtake. He says he's had his week and it's time I started having mine. Queen of Carnelia, here I come!'

Opal shut the book with a snap and a silence fell between the two girls.

The funny thing was that Martha and Opal had never had a proper conversation about the fact that Opal was leaving. They had discussed the obvious things, like how good it was that no one apart from Robbie and Martha had found out Opal was an alien, and how pleased Uncle Bixbite would be when she finally got her CIA. But they had never talked about how they would feel when it came to saying goodbye. Martha didn't really want to talk about it because that would make it all too real. Opal didn't seem to want to talk about it either. Neither of them wanted to admit that their time together was coming to an end.

Martha was accidentally thinking how much she would miss Opal when she finally did go back to Carnelia, when Opal shouted, 'Oh! Oh, my zippedee-zooming-do-dogs! Mrs U is coming. She's all dressed up. And look! She's brought her new Earth hound!' She bounded out of the door.

'Her new dog? Has she?' Martha rushed after her. She had been dying to meet Mrs Underedge's new dog. She had told them all about her but this was their first chance to see her.

'Hello, dears.' The teacher looked hot and a bit sweaty. She was wearing the grey suit she always wore to school, but she had tucked a flowery tablecloth into the waistband of her trousers and tied lots of scarves to her jacket sleeves.

'Greetings, Mrs U,' said Opal. 'I like that get-up you've got up in!'

'Thank you, Opal.' Mrs Underedge bowed stiffly. 'Gypsy Rose Underedge at your service. Sorry I'm a little late. I had quite a job packing the parachute silk into this travelling bag. Nevertheless, it should be useful for our purposes.' Big clumps of yellow material stuck out of a bag on wheels she was pulling behind her. Martha recognised the school parachute.

They used it for PE games in the hall, when it was too wet to go outside.

A scarf which Mrs Underedge had wrapped round her head slipped down over her glasses. She let go of the bag to adjust it, all the time keeping a tight hold of the lead in her other hand. On the end of the lead was the cutest dog Martha had ever seen. Its coat was patched cream and soft brown; it had adorable dark brown eyes and a pretty pale blue collar.

'She's so sweet!' said Martha.

'Sit, Bonnie-Belle-Flower-Lady!' commanded Mrs Underedge. 'You have visitors.'

The dog sat down at once and waited politely to be petted. She had the silkiest snout, and her long ears were like velvet.

'She's a pedigree, actually,' said Mrs Underedge proudly. 'Quite valuable. If she had puppies they could be worth a great deal of money.'

'Bonnie-Belle-Flower-Lady,' said Opal. 'That's a name and three-quarters!'

'Ah, well,' said Mrs Underedge, 'it was a terribly difficult decision. Bonnie and Belle, Flower and Lady were all on the shortlist, and I simply couldn't choose between them. In the end I thought, oh blow it, I'll have them all! Bonnie-Belle-Flower-Lady. It suits her, don't you think?'

'It sounds like the name of a princess,' said Martha, stroking Bonnie-Belle-Flower-Lady under the chin. The dog looked a bit like a princess, too. It was something to do with the way she raised her head and allowed you to stroke her, as if she was doing you a favour, and not the other way around.

'Such a good little companion,' said Mrs Underedge. 'I don't know how I ever managed without her.' She bent down and patted Bonnie-Belle-Flower-Lady while Martha tickled her ears.

'The most beauteous pooch I've seen in a long while,' agreed Opal, sounding a little bored. Martha could tell she was impatient for the Fete to begin. 'Now, what do you think of this, Mrs U?' She skipped over to her popcorn sign and held it up for Mrs Underedge to see.

'Goodness!' said Mrs Underedge. 'That is impressive, Opal. Excellent. I can see I shall have to recruit you for scenery-making when we start work on next year's play.'

A pang of sadness went through Martha as she remembered that Opal wouldn't be around for the next school play. Opal's year on Earth had passed so quickly. Martha didn't know where the time had gone.

'Time dies when you're having fun,' said Opal, as if to answer her thoughts.

'I beg your pardon, Opal, dear?' Mrs Underedge looked puzzled.

Martha was just about to say something to cover up for Opal's strange statement when she heard a *chia-wa chia-wo chia-wo-wow* coming from the Domestipod.

24

She turned to see Garnet, who had woken up and was now parading smartly up and down the window ledge. His stubby lynx tail was sticking up as high as it would go. His amber eyes were wide open and fixed firmly on Mrs Underedge's dog.

Bonnie-Belle-Flower-Lady watched Garnet, her head on one side, ears raised questioningly. Then she yawned and looked away, letting her gaze rest on a nearby lamp post.

Garnet stood on his hind legs and strutted about, showing off the spots and stripes on his belly. When Bonnie-Belle-Flower-Lady still refused to look at him he began to perform an elaborate little dance. At least, Martha thought he was dancing. He swayed from side to side and made peculiar little running movements with his paws. The dance got faster and faster. Garnet whirled round and round, chasing his tail. Then he went too fast for his own paws, tripped and fell off the ledge into Opal's flowerbed.

Opal snorted with laughter. 'Garnie!' she cried. 'I didn't know you were a ballpark dancer! Was that the foxy-trotter you were doing just then, or the mango?'

'Tango!' Martha said, laughing too. She didn't want to hurt Garnet's feelings, but he looked so funny; even Mrs Underedge blew her nose, which was the nearest she ever came to laughing in the first place. Bonnie-Belle-Flower-Lady opened her mouth and let her tongue loll around over her dainty teeth as if she was grinning at the joke too.

Garnet jumped up to his place on the ledge and stared back at them all. He did look quite offended, cross even. He narrowed his owl eyes until they were slits in his face. A small growl rumbled in his throat.

Then he did something crazy, something that could destroy Opal's chances of getting her CIA and becoming Queen of Carnelia for good.

He whirled his head right round on his shoulders and he spread his flying-fox wings.

3

Martha couldn't believe it. Garnet never opened his wings. Not unless they were alone in the Domestipod with the blind down. He had always taken care to keep his wings and his revolving head a secret so that everyone took him for a funny-looking dog. Instead of what he really was: a mix of six different animals made by Opal in a Minmangulator.

He was usually so sensible. Opal had nearly given away her alien identity a couple of times, but Garnet never had. Now, suddenly, here he was, revolving his head right the way round and opening his bluey-grey wings in broad daylight, for anyone to see.

Bonnie-Belle-Flower-Lady was paying Garnet much more attention now. She was yapping with

excitement and running rings round her mistress's ankles.

Martha glanced at Mrs Underedge, sure that she would be about to scream, or faint even, but Mrs Underedge hadn't noticed Garnet. She was busy disentangling herself from Bonnie-Belle-Flower-Lady's lead, which was wrapped round her legs.

'Stop that, Bonnie-Belle-Flower-Lady!' she said, trying not to topple over. 'Hush, girl! Quiet now!'

Martha saw her chance. She dived for the windowsill and grabbed Garnet. She pressed his wings to his sides and held him tightly under her arm, so that he couldn't open them again.

'*Garnie!*' she hissed. 'What are you *thinking?*'

Chi-chi, Garnet said. He didn't struggle. He sat gazing at Bonnie-Belle-Flower-Lady as she gazed back at him.

'Dear me!' said Mrs Underedge, straightening her glasses. 'I don't know what's come over Bonnie-Belle-Flower-Lady. She's never behaved so disobediently before.' She peered at her watch. 'She'll make us late if we're not careful. Come, girls, let us prepare for our merry fortune-hunters.'

She led the way through the park gates, trundling the bag with the parachute silk behind her.

'That was a tight shave!' Opal whispered.

'I know!' Martha whispered back.

'Fact is,' said Opal, hitching her popcorn sign up a little higher under her arm, 'I think Garnet's taken a bit of a shimmer to Bonnie-Belle-Flower-Lady.'

'You mean, he fancies her?'

'Must do. He never would have put on such a performance otherwise. He must have fallen over for her.'

'Fallen *for* her,' Martha corrected.

'*And* fallen over!' said Opal with a grin.

'I didn't know mingles could fall in love,' said Martha, as Mrs Underedge led them past the Bucking Bronco. A small group was gathered around it already, watching the man slot the bull's body together and then go and plug it in.

'They can't,' said Opal. 'It never happens on Carnelia, anyway. It's not logical, you see. If you ask me, some Earth feelings have been polishing off on our Garnie, and making him behave oddly. He's become extremely unpredictable lately. Even I don't know what he's going to do next.'

'We'd better keep an eye on him, then,' said Martha. Opal was so close to getting her CIA now. And they had done so much to help her get it, making sure she didn't reveal her true identity, finding ways for her to keep Garnet with her at all times so she didn't fade away to nothing. They had even defeated the evil Mercurials when they had come to Earth to prevent Opal from winning the CIA so that they could claim the Carnelian Coronet for themselves. Now there were only three more weeks to go. It would be terrible if Garnet threw the whole thing away for Opal with one silly mistake.

Martha wagged her finger at the mingle. 'That was not the right thing to do, Garnet,' she scolded.

'No,' agreed Opal. 'That was not the right thing at all.'

Garnet gave them an apologetic look and they both patted his head to show they weren't really cross with him.

'Ah, yes. This will do nicely.' Mrs Underedge had stopped by an old flower arch. She reached up and pulled a few dead leaves out of the metalwork. 'A little set-dressing, and Gypsy Rose will be ready for her first clients.'

Opal set up her sign while Martha helped Mrs Underedge drape the yellow parachute silk over the arch. It made a very good tent. Martha went inside it and put out the cushions Mrs Underedge had brought with her.

'Excellent!' said Mrs Underedge, following her in and tying Bonnie-Belle-Flower-Lady's lead to the arch. 'Now I just need my crystal ball—' she took a glass paperweight out of her handbag '—and I shall be ready for my first customers. Martha, do we have a receptacle for the takings?'

Martha waved her margarine tub. 'I thought we could put the money in this,' she said.

'Jolly good.' Mrs Underedge settled herself on a cushion. 'Let me know when someone is ready to cross my palm with silver.'

When Martha found her way out of the parachute silk, Opal was ripping the popcorn off her sign and eating it.

'Sorry, Martha,' she said through a mouthful, 'but I was feeling a bit nibblish. It's OK, though, because the news is travelling by speech of tongue.'

She was right. A queue was forming outside Gypsy Rose Underedge's tent. Everyone wanted to hear what Mrs Underedge would say to them. Opal and Martha made their way along the line, taking money. The margarine tub was soon heavy with silver coins.

Jessie was in the queue, holding a huge glass jar full of sweets. 'I haven't counted them yet,' she said, giving the jar a shake. 'Do you want to guess how many?'

'Three hundred and eighty-seven,' said Opal at once.

Martha trod on her foot. She knew Opal didn't need to guess. With her eyes she could see at once how many sweets were in the jar. They looked delicious but it wouldn't be fair for Opal to win them like that.

A year ago Opal wouldn't have understood. She would have asked Martha why she was standing on her foot and staring at her in such a strange way, but she was much better at taking hints now.

'Oh. Or, actually, on second thinkings, five hundred and four,' said Opal, 'give or take a strawberry chew.'

Jessie wrote the second guess down in her little book.

Martha looked around. The Fun Fete was well under way now, and the park was packed with people.

'Would you like me to take the money for a while,' Jessie offered, 'so you can have a look at what else is going on?'

'Yes, please!' Opal said at once. 'I'm dying to have a go on absolutely everything. I want to have all the fun of the Fete!' As she skipped away like an excited toddler, Martha couldn't help thinking Opal didn't look nearly ready to be queen of an entire planet. Queens were supposed to be serious, but Opal wasn't a bit like that. She was always giggling and laughing and shouting – and she was almost never still. She was lolloping along now, calling out, 'Zippedee zooming-do-dogs! Hooray for today!'

Martha and Jessie exchanged smiles.

'Thanks, Jess,' Martha said. 'We won't be long, I promise.'

Jessie was always doing kind things. Martha would feel terrible when Opal went back to Carnelia, but Jessie would still be here, and that was a big consolation.

When she caught up with her, Opal was poring over Ravi and Tom's Treasure Map. She had a pin in her hand and was about to stab it into the map, right into the trunk of a palm tree. Martha knew Opal would be able to see the X the boys had put on the back of the map to mark the spot where the treasure was.

'What about under that barrel of rum?' she suggested quickly. 'That would be a good place for the treasure. It's all about *guessing*, isn't it, Opal?'

'Oh!' said Opal. 'I see! It's a *guessing* game. And that's a much better guess than mine was. Thanks, Martha.' She stuck her pin in the barrel and handed over her money.

'Trust you to keep me on the straight and marrows, Martha,' she said as they wandered away. 'If I get my CIA on the twenty-sixth of August it'll all be down to you. You always help me do the right thing.'

She stopped short. 'Now, what *is* going on over there?'

Martha followed her gaze and saw Sam, balancing on a tree stump in his vest and tracksuit bottoms. He was completely drenched, water dripping from his nose and chin. A crowd of boys, including Robbie, were lobbing soaking-wet sponges at him. Sam was holding out his arms and grinning. He caught Martha's eye and waved, but she pretended she hadn't seen him. She already saw quite enough of Sam at home.

'Now *that* looks like fun,' said Opal.

'Don't you have sponge-throwing on your planet?'

Martha steered Opal away. She didn't want to throw sponges at Sam. It would be far too embarrassing. 'What about crockery-smashing,' she said, pointing to another stall. 'Or welly-wanging. Do you have either of those?'

'We most certainly do not,' said Opal. 'We're not supposed to have fun like that on Carnelia. Uncle Bixie's been stamping down on it. He's even stopped people going asteroid-riding.'

'Asteroid-riding?'

'I know,' said Opal. 'How harsh is that? He says it's all far too amusing, and not a bit logical. Uncle Bixie can be very strict.'

Did that mean Opal would have to be strict too, when she ruled over Carnelia? Martha couldn't picture that at all.

'Oh, I'll be so strict and stern,' Opal answered, leapfrogging over a bush. 'I'll be as tough as old snails!'

Martha laughed. 'I doubt it,' she said, leapfrogging after her.

'Hello, girls. How's Gypsy Rose getting on?'

It was Mum, standing by the wig stall she and Alesha were running. Alesha had decided that A Cut Above needed to branch out. Now, as well as doing haircuts at the salon, she and Mum were selling hair extensions and wigs.

'Hi, Mum. It's going really well.'

'Yes, thank you, Marie Stephens,' said Opal. She

35

always gave Mum her full name. 'Mrs U has made a bomb-load of money already.'

'More than we have,' complained Alesha, waving at her display. 'We've hardly sold any of these wigettos at all. That's the trouble with Archwell. No one has any sense of fashion.'

'I'm sure sales will pick up soon,' said Mum.

'Whatever.' Alesha sniffed. 'I'm off to Italy on Monday for my holidayini, so I couldn't care less. You never know, I might not come back. I might fall in love with a handsome Italiano man. I might sell up and stay out there forever.'

Martha caught Mum's eye. Alesha had been saying things like this ever since she had booked her holiday. Martha was quite worried because if she did sell the salon, Mum would be out of a job. But Alesha often talked like this, and Mum's smile reminded Martha of what she always told her. It was best to take Alesha with a pinch of salt.

And there were far more exciting things to think about. She could see Opal, already at the ice-cream stall, buying two giant cornets.

'Can't stop,' she said, giving Mum a wave as she ran to join her.

'Frozen explosion?' Opal handed her a cornet coated with thick chocolate sauce. 'Now come on, Martha. Let's party! Let's do everything there is to do. Let's go stark raving fruit and nuts!'

Martha and Opal ran through the Fete, racing from stall to stall, stopping now and again to lick ice cream from their hands.

And they did do everything – everything apart from sponge throwing, anyway. They lobbed wellies, smashed crockery, threw balls into buckets, guessed the name of a teddy, hooked plastic ducks from a paddling pool and and bounced up and down on the bouncy castle until they felt sick. They were too big for the bouncy castle – it was really for little kids – but Opal wanted to give it a try. In fact, she wanted to give it about thirty tries.

It was while they were bouncing that Martha noticed Jessie walking by. With a pang of guilt she realised it had been ages since they had left her in

charge of taking money at the fortune-telling stall. She must be looking for them.

'Jessie!' she called. 'I'm so sorry. We'll come back right now.'

'It's OK,' Jessie called back. 'Chloe and Colette have taken over. I'm going to see the Bucking Bronco. It's closing in a minute. You coming?'

'Yes, we are!' cried Opal, careering off the bouncy castle at last. 'I wouldn't miss the Bucking Bronco for anything, not for all the tea in a china teacup!'

She grabbed Martha and Jessie's hands and the three of them ran off together.

They reached the arena just in time to see Robbie, wearing a cowboy hat and waistcoat, being thrown off the Bucking Bronco machine. He took off the hat and waistcoat and handed them to the girl behind him.

'It's completely impossible to hold on,' he panted, joining them by the fence. 'Fifteen seconds is the record so far. Ravi did that. I did ten, but I reckon I'd have managed longer if I didn't bite my fingernails. Maybe Sam can do better.'

'Sam?'

To Martha's dismay, Sam was next in the queue. Everyone else lining up was under twelve. He towered over them all, sticking out like a sore thumb. He was still wet, too, from having so many sponges thrown at him.

Ravi sat on the fence, waiting to see if anyone

would equal his record. 'Who is that guy?' he asked as Sam spat on his hands and prepared to mount the Bronco. 'Is he your dad?'

'No, he is not!' said Martha. She and Robbie had a perfectly good dad already. They didn't get to see him very often because he lived quite a long way away, but he wasn't a bit like Sam.

'Who is he, then?' said Ravi.

'A swimming instructor, I think.' Martha tried to sound vague. She didn't want people thinking Sam was connected to her in any way.

'Yes, and he's going out with our mum,' Robbie announced. 'He's her new man!'

Ravi grinned. 'Cool!'

'Sam the Man!' said Opal, savouring the words.

Martha could just tell she was going to call Sam that all the time from now on. 'Thanks a lot, Robbie,' she muttered.

'Yee*haaa*!' yelled Sam as he mounted the bull. The waistcoat was much too small for him and the cowboy hat looked ridiculous, perched on his big head. He raised one hand in the air as the Bronco started to move, shouted, 'Ride 'em, cowboy!' and then immediately toppled sideways. His foot caught in one of the stirrups as he fell, so he had to crawl away awkwardly on his hands. He laughed up at Mum, who was leaning over the fence to see if he was hurt. 'Howdy, pardner!' he said in a stupid American accent.

Martha felt herself going red with embarrassment. 'He acts like such a big kid!' she mumbled as Jessie went to take her turn on the Bronco.

'What's wrong with big kids?' Opal sounded genuinely curious.

'Well, nothing, but—'

'Martha! Opal! Have you seen Bonnie-Belle-Flower-Lady?'

Mrs Underedge scurried towards them, shedding scarves and wringing her hands.

'I think she must have slipped her lead, I don't know when. I was so involved in my fortune-telling, I didn't see her go!'

Martha hadn't seen Bonnie-Belle-Flower-Lady, not since they had left the fortune-telling stall. Looking round, she realised that she hadn't seen Garnet for a while either. He wasn't in any of his usual places, on Opal's head or in her pocket or in the waistband of her shorts. She glanced quickly at Opal. If Opal ever lost sight of Garnet, she started to fade away at once. Without him she could even die. But Opal's shining, happy face, the relaxed way she was perching on the fence, told Martha that Garnet couldn't be far away.

'Oh, not to worry, Mrs U,' Opal said. 'There's no need to get your pants in a palaver. Bonnie-Belle-Flower-Lady is over there, with Garnet, in those eternally green trees!'

She pointed to some evergreen bushes that edged the park.

'In the *rhododendrons*?' Mrs Underedge eyed the bushes as if they were the deepest, darkest woods and full of danger. 'Are you sure?'

'Yes, look,' Opal said. 'I've been watching them for a while. They've been having a great time. They've been having a balloon!'

'Ball,' corrected Martha as she saw Garnet rush out of the bushes. Bonnie-Belle-Flower-Lady scampered after him, barking excitedly. The two of them went roly-polying away and then got up and licked each other's faces, both their tails wagging like mad.

'Oh! Oh dear!' said Mrs Underedge as the two now very dusty animals danced round each other in a circle, nose to nose.

Martha didn't think Mrs Underedge looked too happy about Bonnie-Belle-Flower-Lady's new friendship, so she picked the little dog up and handed her over. She felt grubby and her collar was sticky, as if she had been rolling in candyfloss.

'Thank you, Martha,' said Mrs Underedge, holding Bonnie-Belle-Flower-Lady slightly away from her white shirt. 'I am grateful. However, this has been a most trying experience. I have a headache. I think Bonnie-Belle-Flower-Lady and I will go home now for some relaxation. A nice cup of coffee and a spot of mental maths should do the trick.'

Only Mrs Underedge, Martha thought, picking up her scarves for her. No one else would do maths to help them relax.

'I wonder, Opal,' the teacher said, fishing a lead out of her handbag, 'I really have so little strength left today, could you perhaps look after the school parachute silk for me? I don't think I can manage it now. I could collect it from your little house in a few days' time, if that would be convenient.'

'Of course, Mrs U,' said Opal. 'I'd be happy to be helpful.' She was fidgeting about in the queue, desperate for her turn on the Bucking Bronco.

'We'll get the silk down off the arch for you too,' said Martha.

'What good girls you are.' Mrs Underedge attached the lead to Bonnie-Belle-Flower-Lady's collar. 'Well, I've done my bit. I'm sure the new skateboard bowl will be an excellent resource for young people, and provide plenty of fresh air and exercise.'

With that, she set off slowly through the park, muttering maths problems under her breath.

Bonnie-Belle-Flower-Lady kept her head turned, staring back at Garnet as she was led away. She barked two short, delicate barks, which Garnet answered with a farewell *chi-cha*.

'What do you mean, she's the last?'

Opal was talking to the Bucking Bronco man, who had just let Jessie through to the Bronco.

'I've got another gig in Camberhill after this,' the man explained as Jessie climbed up. 'You'll have to give it a miss this time, love.'

'I most certainly will not give it a miss!' said Opal.

'Not on your Nellie the elephant! I'm sorry, Mr Bronco man, but this is my very first Earth Fete, and it will be my last. So it wouldn't be fair to stop me from having a buck on your zooming bronco, now would it, please?'

The man seemed surprised to be spoken to like this. He glanced at Martha.

She smiled at him. 'Pretty please?' she said.

'Beautiful please?' said Opal. 'Most magnificent and marvellous please? Please with frills and bells and lacy bits?'

'All right, all right,' said the man. 'Keep your hair on, you can have a go. But you're the very last.' He took Opal's coin and zipped it away in his money belt.

'Yippee!' cried Opal as she leaped the fence. Then she leaped back and danced over to Martha.

'Do you mind if I have the last go, Best Friend in the Universe?' she said.

'No,' Martha said. 'It's fine.' She knew she would have other chances to go on a Bucking Bronco. Besides, when Opal called her Best Friend in the Universe she couldn't refuse her anything.

Opal galloped away, swung herself onto the plastic bull and took hold of the reins.

'Holding tight?' the man said, his finger hovering over the start button. 'Ready?'

'Aim! Fire!' said Opal.

The man pressed the button and the bull whirred into life. It swayed from side to side. It jiggled and lurched. Opal stayed on. Then it bucked. Its rump tipped abruptly upwards, flinging Opal forwards, then backwards, then sideways. She stayed on.

The Bucking Bronco man was looking at his watch. He pressed another button and the bull bucked faster and harder, jerking in all directions. It had no effect. Opal balanced perfectly. She balanced on the bull as easily as Garnet balanced on her head.

Everyone in the crowd went *ooh* and *aah*.

Opal loved being the centre of attention. She soaked up attention the way some people soak up the sun. She let go of the reins and raised her arms in the air. Then she actually stood up on the bull's back, and as if that wasn't enough, she lifted a foot and balanced on one leg. She looked as calm and stable as a plastic ballet dancer standing on a smoothly iced cake. Where did she learn to balance like that? Martha wondered.

'I was Champion Asteroid Rider three years running,' Opal called back to her as everyone laughed and cheered her on. They thought she was joking.

Opal whooped. 'Rock 'n' rule!' she shouted. 'Rock 'n' rule!'

Robbie cupped his hands to his mouth and yelled, 'Rock 'n' *roll*, you mean!'

Opal waved the cowboy hat at him.

The man, fed up with waiting, switched the machine off and the bull chugged to a halt. Martha half expected to see steam come out of its ears. It didn't, but it still had a defeated look about it, as if Opal had tamed it in one quick session. The Bronco man looked a bit defeated too. He wanted to take his machine apart and put it away, but he couldn't get to it because of the crowd gathered round Opal, clapping and exclaiming and reaching up to shake her hands.

Martha smiled to herself. One down on her Summer Schedule of Stuff To Do, nine to go. And they still had twenty more whole days before Opal had to go back to Carnelia. Martha was going to make the absolute most of them. They didn't need to do much. They could go to the mini-market for ice lollies, cool their feet in the little kids' paddling pool, make popcorn. Nothing special. They'd do all the things they'd done last summer; all the things that Opal had loved doing then. The main thing was that they would be together.

'Good plan, Martha,' Opal shouted over the heads of the crowd. 'I like it. From now on, we'll stick to each other like goo!'

Martha laughed. Sometimes it was very handy having a friend who could read minds.

And then, in that happy moment, the thought of Number 10 swam up into her mind. Number 10 on her Summer Schedule.

10. Say goodbye to Opal Moonbaby forever

Number 10 was going to be the most difficult thing she would ever have to do in her life. She was dreading saying goodbye. She looked at Opal's amazing violet eyes and imagined, so very clearly, what it would be like to look into them for the very last time. She wished it didn't have to happen.

I can't even do it, she thought as she stared at Opal. I can't go through with it. I'd rather die than say goodbye to you, Opal Moonbaby.

Martha saw Opal blink twice before a band of admirers lifted her down from the Bronco and she sank into the crowd. Martha lost sight of her.

She wouldn't let that happen again. From now on, Martha was determined not to be parted from Opal for one more second than was absolutely necessary. She would make sure they were together all day, every day, until the last day of all.

5

'What? No! We *can't* be!'

Martha dropped her spoon into her bowl.

'Martha,' said Mum. 'I thought you'd be pleased about going camping. It was meant to be a lovely surprise.'

'I'm pleased,' said Robbie, scooping Space Nuggets into his mouth. 'I can't wait. Sam's told me all about the campsite. It's on a cliff right above the sea, so we can go to the beach every day. There's a zip-wire in the trees, and they let you have campfires and toast marshmallows and stuff. It's going to be so slick!'

Martha kept her eyes fixed on the table. 'Where is this campsite?'

'West Wales,' said Mum. 'About a five-hour drive away.'

Five hours! Martha gave her bowl a shove. It clanged against the milk bottle. If they were going that far, she'd never get to see Opal at all! She might as well be back on Carnelia already.

'I'm not going. I want to stay here!' She felt panicky, as if she might be about to cry. She fixed her face into a scowl to stop the tears from coming.

'I don't understand you, Martha.' Mum dabbed at a patch of milk that had landed on her shirt. 'I thought you'd love camping. It never crossed my mind you wouldn't want to go. I said yes as soon as Sam suggested it. He's booked it already. It's such superb timing, too. Alesha's closing the salon tomorrow for her trip to Italy, so for once I won't have to work. It'll be so nice to have a little family holiday.'

'Sam's not family,' said Martha quickly.

'No,' Mum looked embarrassed, 'you're right, he's not. Family *apart* from Sam, I mean. But it's very kind of him to offer to take us, and we couldn't do it without him. He's the one with the tent, after all.'

'How long are we supposed to stay there?' Martha knew she sounded ungrateful but she couldn't help it. It was such a shock.

'Well, Alesha's shut the salon for two weeks and the campsite's got a free pitch, so if the weather holds we can go for a whole fortnight.'

'Oh yea-ah, oh yea-ah!' sang Robbie, jiggling a mini-victory dance on his chair.

Martha did a calculation in her head. If she went away for a fortnight now, she would only have six days left with Opal after that. It wasn't nearly enough. There wouldn't even be time to do all the things on the Summer Schedule. Mum was right – she didn't understand. She didn't understand that she was ripping away more than half of the precious time Martha had left with Opal.

Martha couldn't explain, either. Mum didn't even know Opal was an alien, so she couldn't say she had to stay at home because Opal was going back to her planet on the twenty-sixth of August. She racked her brain for some other solution.

'Can Opal come too?' she said as one came to her, filling her with new hope. If she had to go on holiday, she could take Opal with her.

Mum shook her head. 'There wouldn't be room in the car,' she said. 'Or the tent.'

The hope flitted away as quickly as it had arrived, but Martha couldn't just give up.

'I'll stay here, then. I'll stay and keep Opal company.'

'No, Martha.' Mum frowned. 'You can see your friend when you get back.' She started clearing the breakfast things. 'You're coming with us. You'll love it when you get there.'

Her phone rang. 'Oh, it's Sam,' she said, blushing as his name appeared on the screen. 'He's coming over in half an hour. We're all going to the camping shop to get a few bits and bobs we need.'

Martha watched as Mum disappeared into her bedroom with her mobile. Mum had absolutely no idea what this was doing to her. She was so busy with Sam these days, she hardly noticed what Martha was feeling.

She turned to Robbie, who was taking the opportunity to help himself to extra Space Nuggets.

'What is *up* with you?' Martha said. 'Have you forgotten that Opal and Garnet are going back to Carnelia? We'll never see them again, you know. Don't you want to stay with them?'

'Well, yes,' said Robbie. 'But they'll still be here when we get back from camping, won't they?'

'Only for a week. Six days, in fact. And then they'll be gone. Forever. Don't you care about that?'

Robbie squirmed in his chair. 'I do,' he said, taking Yoyo, his old and now very faded monkey from his pocket and balancing him on top of the Space Nuggets box. ''Course I do. I love Garnet, and Opal's fantastic, but the thing is, Martha, I haven't been to the beach for centuries, and I've never been camping before, ever. Not in my whole entire life. Sam said he'd teach me to dive.'

'Oh, Sam, Sam, Sam!' Martha said. She knew she was being unkind, but Sam was all Mum and Robbie ever talked about at the moment.

'No need to be like that, Martha,' Robbie said, using the same voice Mum used when she told him off. He made Yoyo do a somersaulting dive off the cereal box. 'Yesss! Yoyo Stephens dives into the Welsh sea and smashes the world record! It's un-be-lievable!' He swam the monkey across the table.

Martha could see she wasn't going to get anywhere with Robbie. She stomped into the corridor and searched the shoe pile for her flip-flops. Sam had left a pair of his pongy trainers there again. They made her feel sick. She could hear Mum chatting to him on the phone, discussing what they would need to take on the camping trip.

'Oh yes, they've both got sleeping bags. And I've got an old duvet I can bring. Can't wait!'

Martha rammed her feet so hard into her flip-flops that the rubber hurt the skin between her toes. Mum hadn't even asked her if she wanted to go away. She'd just gone and arranged it all with Sam, behind her back. This wasn't the first time something like this had happened. The day after term had ended, Martha had been about to go and see Opal when Mum and Sam announced they were going to the zoo for the day. She liked the zoo, she'd loved the animals, but that wasn't the point. Mum should have asked her about it first. It wasn't fair. This wasn't fair, either!

Martha went out, slamming the door behind her.

She and Opal would have to make a plan, she thought, as she ran down the stairs. Find a way to be together. Run away if necessary. They had only been parted for a day when Martha had gone to the zoo, but they couldn't be parted for a whole two weeks. Not now. It was impossible. Opal would understand. Opal would see it her way.

✗ ✗ ✗

Opal was in a strange mood. She had a mini-market carrier bag tied round her head and she was doing something Martha had never seen her do before.

She was cleaning. She had buckets and mops all over the place and was down on her knees, scrubbing the floor. The Domestipod was ankle-deep in foam.

The beanbags they usually sat on looked a bit damp, so Martha sloshed through the bubbly water and perched on a stool instead.

Opal didn't look up. She just kept scrubbing. Garnet was crouching in his hammock, watching her through its strings. His head revolved slowly, his eyes following her round the room.

'What's going on?'

'Summer cleaning,' said Opal, wringing out the cloth, which Martha now saw was one of Opal's floppy purple hats. 'Uncle Bixbite's coming to Earth in a few days. He's going to give me a final pepping talk before my Ascendance. He'll want to see the Domestipod looking shopshape, won't he?' She scrubbed at the window, making it squeak like a marker pen being pressed too hard.

Martha winced. 'Will he?' She wanted to talk about the camping trip and how she could get out of it, but it was proving quite difficult to get Opal's attention.

'A clean Carnelian is a complete Carnelian,' said Opal to no one in particular. She glanced at the wall and the shower cubicle came gliding out. She reached inside, pulled out the shower hose and began to spray things. 'Tidy house, tidy brain,' she said to the ceiling as she fired water at it.

Martha didn't know where these sayings had come from. Opal had never used them before. Above her, Garnet flattened his ears in anticipation of a wetting.

One of the beanbags was starting to float. It bobbed over to a large object that was standing right in the middle of the room, draped with one of Opal's purple cloaks.

Martha waded towards it. 'I've never seen this before.' She lifted the cloak a little to reveal a smooth silvery surface. 'Have you bought a new fridge? What is it?'

'It's nothing for nosy pokers!'

Martha jumped as the corner of the cloak crackled like electricity. It flew out of her hand and settled back down on the silvery object, hiding it from view. A shimmer of violet light ran round it and then faded away.

Martha turned and stared at Opal. She had never used her eye power against Martha before. She'd never used it against anyone except the Mercurials, and they were members of an evil Carnelian clan who had been trying to hurt her.

And she seemed so cross. Opal was never normally cross but she looked positively angry now. She had stopped cleaning and was staring hard at Martha. Her eyes glittered with violet sparks. The handles of the carrier bag tied over her eyebrows made her look even angrier. It was like looking at a completely different person. Martha took a step backwards. Her fingers still smarted as if they'd been slapped.

'What did you do that for?'

'Sorry,' Opal said immediately. She pushed the carrier bag up a bit and scratched her forehead. 'I didn't mean it, Martha. I don't know what flew over me.'

She eyed the object hidden under the cloak. 'It's nothing. Nothing at all. Really. It's just something that arrived this morning by special delivery, from Carnelia. It's nothing important. Nothing to trouble your brainy little head with, anyway.'

'OK,' said Martha. 'It's none of my business. You don't have to tell me if you don't want to. I don't mind.'

Although she did mind. They both knew that. An awkward silence fell between them. The only sound came from the shower head, still in Opal's hand, still spewing water like a fountain.

'You know what, Martha?' said Opal at last, her voice oddly bright. 'I think you should go on this camping trip.'

'What?' Martha hadn't even mentioned the camping trip yet, but she realised now that she had been concentrating on it so hard when she came in that Opal had read her thoughts and knew all about it already.

'Yes,' said Opal. 'You should definitely go. I'm sure you'll have a shark of a time.'

Martha frowned. 'I want to stay with you, though, Opal. I want us to be together for your last bit of time on Earth. You want me to stay too, don't you?'

'It would be lovely if you could,' Opal agreed. 'But I don't want to stop you having a holiday. Think of all that frisky sea air you'll have.'

'Oh, Opal,' Martha said, suddenly overwhelmed by a picture of herself and Opal on the beach together. 'I bet you'd love the seaside. You could come too!'

She was about to list all the things there were to do by the sea when Opal said, 'I'm afraid I can't. I'm far too busy getting my house into cherry-pie order. You see, I'm expecting Uncle Bixbite any day. He's coming to give me my marching commands.'

'I know. You said. But couldn't you come for a day or two before that? There's no space in Sam's car, apparently, but maybe you could come by yourself, in the Domestipod.'

She knew that wasn't likely. Uncle Bixbite had given Opal strict instructions never to travel in the Domestipod in case it attracted attention. The only place she was allowed to fly to was the island of Muckle Flugga, where she went when she needed to recharge her eyes. And she could only fly there on cloudless nights. Opal flying to the beach in Wales was a long shot, but it was worth a try. Wasn't it?

'You're clutching at strawberries, I'm afraid, Martha,' said Opal.

'Straws, you mean.'

Martha couldn't understand why Opal was being so awkward. She wasn't even trying to help. Martha wished she could be the one to read thoughts for a change, so she could find out what on earth was going on in Opal's mind.

'Won't you be lonely, all on your own?'

Opal laughed. It wasn't a proper laugh. It was more of a high-pitched whinny, like a horse would make. It grated on Martha's ears.

'Noo-oooo!' Opal said in her new super-cheerful voice. 'We Carnelians are totally self-contained and self-sufficient, you know. We don't need other people. I'll be fine. You go on holiday, Martha. You go and enjoy yourself.'

How could Martha enjoy herself if Opal wasn't there?

'I thought you'd want to spend time together,' she said, trying to catch Opal's eye. 'What's happened to you, Opal? What happened to sticking together like goo? That's what you said we'd do. You said that *yesterday*!'

Opal was looking everywhere except at Martha. She didn't seem to be able to hear her. She dropped the shower head in a bucket where it landed with a splash, grabbed a mop and began knocking at imaginary cobwebs on the ceiling, singing as she did so. It was a song about the sea. Opal was almost shouting it, and it was all out of tune.

Martha felt like giving her a shove. Why couldn't she act normally? Opal's attitude was hurtful enough, but the fact that she could read thoughts and must know how unhappy she was making Martha feel made it all the worse.

Par-parp-p-par-parp!

Opal glanced at the window. 'Oh, look,' she said. 'It's Robbie and Marie Stephens and Sam the Man.'

With a lurch, Martha remembered the shopping trip she was meant to be going on.

'They're rooting and tooting for you, Martha. You'd better go.'

'You can't wait to get rid of me, can you?'

Martha felt as if she'd been stung, not once, but over and over again. Opal had never been unkind like this. Her human friends had been mean to her sometimes, but Opal never had. She didn't know how to be mean. Obviously that had changed now, though.

'All right,' said Martha. 'If that's what you want, I will. I *will* go!'

'Have a super time, won't you?' said Opal. 'Here, let me open the door for you.' She flashed her eyes and the green door slid open.

Martha rushed towards it. She was almost outside when Opal called out, 'Martha, wait!'

'What?' Martha turned and Opal looked her in the eyes at last. Her violet eyes seemed to soften, and Martha thought she was going to take everything back, change her mind, beg Martha to find a way to stay behind in Archwell with her.

But then Opal looked away again. She whisked a duster from her pocket and blew her nose on it.

'What a lot of dust I've collected in my nasal passages!' she said, speaking in the ridiculous false voice again. She smiled into the duster. 'You will send me a postcard, won't you, Martha?'

A postcard.

Martha swallowed. 'I'll think about it.'

'How super-smashingly-fantabulously lovely of you,' said Opal. She didn't sound as if she thought any of that, though. She sounded mechanical, the way text messages sounded when people accidentally sent them to the home phone. She sounded as if she didn't have any feelings at all.

She fluttered the duster and said, 'The future Queen of Carnelia wishes you a very sweet and *bonbon voyage!*'

Suddenly Martha felt furious. Opal was acting as if their year together, all their adventures, had never happened, as if they hadn't become as close as it was possible for two people to become. It was as if Opal didn't know all of Martha's thoughts and wishes and secrets. Well, she wouldn't know them any longer; she didn't deserve to.

'Actually, no!' Martha said fiercely, 'I won't send you a postcard. There isn't any point. Because I don't send postcards to . . . to robots!'

She turned on her heel. Mum and Sam and Robbie were waving at her to hurry up and get in the car. She didn't want to go, but there was absolutely no point staying where she was. Opal didn't seem to have the first idea how much she had hurt her feelings. Martha was outraged. She wanted to hurt Opal back. She rounded on her and spat out her words.

'And I'll tell you something else, Opal Moonbaby. There's no way you're ready to be a queen. You'll make a totally *rubbish* one!'

Without waiting for an answer, she ran off to the waiting car, hurled herself onto the back seat and slammed the door. The car moved off and she didn't look back.

The car bounced over the field, rocking Martha around, making her feel sick.

'Here we are, guys!' Sam jumped out and clapped his hands together. 'Get a load of that sea air.'

Mum and Robbie got out of the car too and looked round eagerly. Neither of them seemed to care about the wind or the rain that was flinging itself into their faces.

Sam caught hold of the car door to stop it blowing shut. 'This holiday is going to be extreme!' he said, smiling in at Martha.

Martha smiled back, but she didn't let her eyes join in. She couldn't see what was going to be so *extreme* about the holiday. It had been boiling hot in Archwell, but it was freezing here.

She needed the toilet, but she decided to stay in the car as a protest. She watched Sam padding about all over the field with the farmer and her old dog, looking for a spot flat enough to pitch the tent.

She wished she was still in Archwell. If it hadn't been for Sam, they would never have had to leave home in the first place. It was his idea to set off at the crack of dawn, too, so they could beat the traffic.

Martha had thought Opal might have been meaning to come and talk to her that morning. She might have explained her strange behaviour, apologised even. But they'd left so early, she wouldn't have had the chance. No one had been about when they had driven away from the Half Moon Estate. The whole of Archwell was asleep, and when Martha had peered back over the camping gear, the Domestipod blind was still firmly closed.

Finally Sam settled on a place, and Mum made Martha get out of the car and help. She and Robbie lugged over the tent poles. Martha worked slowly on purpose and Robbie made three trips for every one of hers. He and Mum seemed to be really enjoying it. Mum's cheeks had gone all rosy in the wind, and she was laughing lots. She didn't even complain when one of the tent poles she and Sam were struggling with sprang backwards in the wind and hit her on the leg. A lump came up on her shin, as big as a fat grape, but she didn't seem to mind, just rubbed it and carried on trying to hold up the poles against the wind.

Martha glared at Sam, who put his hands up as if she had pointed a gun at him.

'I know,' he said. 'It's all my fault. I'm sorry.'

They got the tent up eventually and brought the sleeping mats and their night things in from the car. Sam and Mum had one sleeping compartment. Robbie and Martha had the other. What kind of a holiday was it, thought Martha, if you still had to share a room with your little brother? The sleeping space was even smaller than their room at home.

Robbie had a huge bag, which he began to unpack, stashing Yoyo, his packet of playing cards and his new torch in the side pockets of the tent.

'This is so extreme!' he said, heaving out his *Guinness Book of World Records* and putting it under his pillow.

Martha was about to tell him not to start saying *extreme* all the time, because if he and Sam were both doing it, it would drive her mad, when she saw what Robbie was pulling out of his bag. *Eight* of his burst footballs!

'What are *those* doing here?'

'I only brought a selection,' said Robbie. 'To make me feel at home.'

'Ridiculous!' Martha pushed her way out of the sleeping compartment. Not only had she been forced to leave home against her will, but now all the worst bits of home were coming with her. She stormed out of the tent.

Sam was outside, setting up a camping stove. Martha hurried away from him. She needed to be on her own.

'Ow!'

She stumbled over a tent peg and went hopping towards the edge of the cliff, rubbing her foot. It was still raining. Sam had probably found the one place in the entire country that wasn't basking in sunshine.

Behind her, Robbie said, 'Hey, Sam, one of these balls is still OK. Fancy a game of footie?'

'Sure,' said Sam. 'Martha? Do you want to play?'

Martha pretended she hadn't heard. Maybe Sam would think his voice had blown away from her on the salty breeze. Maybe he would think she was being rude and tell Mum about it. She didn't care.

She stood behind the little fence that stopped people from going too close to the edge and looked out to sea.

Clouds were still gathered over the campsite, and Martha could feel her hair going frizzy as a damp mizzle settled on her head. But on the horizon the evening sun had broken free of the clouds and was glowing orange, the sky around it fading from blue to pink.

She was standing at the top of a headland that jutted out into the ocean. On one side of the headland she could see a path zigzagging down to a broad beach. The beach wasn't pebbly as she had expected, but white and sandy, almost tropical. The tiny waves breaking frothily on the smooth sand did look very inviting.

'Penalty!'

'Goal!'

Martha stared at the glittering ocean. She didn't know why she hadn't looked before. Now that she was here, she couldn't tear her eyes away. She hadn't expected it all to be so pretty.

'Three nil!'

'Aw, *referee*!'

Seagulls wafted effortlessly over the water. Three children were at the water's edge, trying to launch a rubber dinghy. Their dog paddled ahead of them, its head sticking up out of the water as it barked encouragement.

Martha smiled. Opal would love it here.

It was with a pang that she realised she was thinking of Opal again. She couldn't help it.

'And he scores!' she heard Robbie boast. 'Just before the final whistle, too!'

Martha crouched down and snapped off a dandelion clock. She watched as the wind snatched at the seeds and they flew away from her, leaving her with just the stalk. She twisted it round her fingers.

'Help me, Martha!' Sam jogged over, putting his hands on his knees while he caught his breath. 'I need another defender on my team.'

'No thanks. I'm a bit tired, actually.'

Why wouldn't he just leave her alone?

'No worries. Maybe next time. Getting your bearings, are you?'

'Yes.'

Martha turned away and looked over to the other side of the headland. There was no path on that side, and the drop down was even steeper. It made Martha feel dizzy, the way she felt when she went to the very top of their block of flats and looked out over Archwell. She took a step backwards but she didn't stop looking. The sea came in much further on that side of the headland, into a small cove the shape of a horseshoe. There wasn't much beach, just a thin strip of white sand.

'That's Nohaven,' Sam said. 'It's not a swimming beach, though, and there's no way down to it from here.'

Martha nodded slightly but she didn't answer. She was curious about the little cove but she hadn't asked Sam to tell her about it. She didn't want him telling her things all the time.

'Uh-oh!' Sam grinned back at Robbie. 'Looks like your brother's scored about a million goals. I'd better get back. Tea's ready in a minute. We're having a fry-up.'

Sam ran off. Martha stayed staring out to sea until the smell of frying bacon reminded her she was hungry and drew her back to the tent.

7

'And this delicious stuff,' said Sam, waving a scraggy greenish-yellow thing under Martha's nose, 'is rock samphire.'

It was the third day of the holiday, and they were on yet another of Sam's foraging and beachcombing expeditions. They were surrounded by things they'd collected: mussels prised from the rocks, a cuttlefish shell, a dead starfish and disgusting-looking squishy things called whelks that Sam had dug up out of the sand. Martha had never known there were so many weird things to find by the sea. She and Robbie probably wouldn't have found half of them if Sam hadn't been with them. Martha was quite interested in all the stuff, but she didn't want to let Sam know that. She hadn't forgiven him yet for

bringing her here.

'You can't eat that!' Martha made a face. The sprig in Sam's hand looked like gone-off broccoli to her.

'Can too.' Sam bit into the sprig and tore some off with his teeth. 'This stuff is gold.'

'Wow!' said Robbie.

'Gold?' Martha doubted it. 'It stinks, like petrol. What's gold about it?'

'Glad you asked me that,' said Sam as he munched. 'It's a superfood. Packed with vitamins. Eating a bit of this could cure you of practically anything. If you were trapped on an island I bet this samphire would save your life, as long as you had some fresh water to wash it down.'

Martha sniffed again at the plant. She was impressed that Sam knew so much about it. She wasn't going to say so, though.

'Cool,' said Robbie. 'Can we go and buy some flags now, Sam, for Castle Extreme?' Sam and Robbie had spent the morning building an enormous sandcastle with a load of turrets.

'Sure,' Sam said. 'Coming, Martha? We could do with an extra pair of hands.'

'No thanks. I've got a postcard to write.'

Martha went to join Mum, who was lying out on her towel, reading a paperback book. She'd been doing that every day. They had arrived in Stormhaven in wind and rain, but it had been really warm ever since.

'Who needs Italy, eh?' Mum reached for the suncream and slathered it on her legs. It smelt fruity and sweet, like melons. 'I hope Alesha's having a good time, but I bet it can't be any lovelier than this.'

Martha didn't answer. She picked up her bag and took out the postcard she had bought in the Stormhaven post office. She hadn't meant to buy the postcard at all – she had told Opal she wasn't going to send her one, but it had sort of slipped into the basket along with their other shopping. She had been trying to keep Opal out of her mind but it was proving very difficult. They'd been apart for four whole days now, and even though Opal had upset her, Martha still found herself wanting to see her.

Just because she had bought the postcard didn't mean she had to write it. It was a bit crushed now, though you could still see the picture of the beach on it. The words *Wish You Were Here* were printed in white on the blue sea. Martha turned it over. She picked up a pen and wrote.

Dear Opal.

Just because she was writing it didn't mean she had to send it. She couldn't think what to put next, anyway. There was plenty she would like to say to Opal, but none of it would fit on the back of a measly postcard.

She flicked the card away onto the sand and hugged her knees.

'Oh, Martha,' said Mum. 'I hope you're going to drop this gloomy act soon. It's been going on for days. You've made your point. Now, can't you start enjoying yourself?'

'I am enjoying myself,' said Martha. She pressed her cheek onto her knee.

'Well, it doesn't seem like it to me,' said Mum. She moved her towel up next to Martha's so they were sitting closer together. 'Look. Is this all about Sam?'

'No.'

'You don't mind me having a boyfriend, do you?'

'No. Of course not.'

She did mind. A while ago Martha had thought how nice it would be for Mum to have a boyfriend, but it was only when Sam came along that she had realised what a big effect it would have on them all. Sam changed everything. The things they did. The way they were with each other. She felt further away from Mum with him around, and further away from Robbie, but there was nothing she could do to stop it. Mum really liked Sam, and it was her life.

'You can go out with whoever you like. It's none of my business.'

'Well, it is your business, in a way. I want you to get on well with Sam. I know Robbie does. But I want you to, too. I don't want you to be unhappy.'

This was a conversation Martha didn't want to

have. There were lots of thoughts in her head but she didn't want to say any of them out loud to Mum. It was too big a subject, somehow. She stood up. 'I'm going for a paddle.'

'All right,' said Mum with a sigh. 'Good idea.' She snapped the lid shut on the suncream, adjusted her sunglasses and settled down with her book again.

✳ ✳ ✳

The water was so cold it made Martha gasp. The ridged sand felt bumpy beneath her feet. A wave lapped over her knees, inviting her in.

She jumped easily over the next couple of waves and then waded out further. A few more steps, and the beach banked sharply away. Before she knew it, she was up to her waist, her top half warm in the sun, her bottom half stony cold and almost numb in the deep water.

Bobbing on her toes, she swivelled round to look up the beach. Above her she could see the campsite on the clifftop. She could see Sam's big blue tent, nestled in among the green and beige ones.

Lowering her gaze, she saw Sam himself. He was carrying two polystyrene cups and had a newspaper shoved under his arm. Robbie ran ahead of him with an ice lolly and a paper bag, which Martha guessed held a bunch of flags. Mum sat up and Sam passed her one of the cups, kissing her cheek as he did so. Anyone else watching them now would think they were a happy little family of three; they would never know that Martha was missing from the scene. They wouldn't know she even existed.

Martha tipped herself backwards until she was lying on top of the water and couldn't see them any more. She floated like that for a while with nothing to look at but the blue sky, a few wisps of cloud and a couple of seagulls gliding around overhead. It would be fun to be a seagull, she thought. If she were a seagull she could fly back to Archwell right now and no one could stop her. She'd probably be there by lunchtime. Then she could find Opal and make her tell her what was wrong. She let out a whining cry of her own, answering the high-pitched calls of the gulls. 'Whaya, whaya whayaaa!'

She felt a sudden need to do something very energetic, so she wheeled her arms round and kicked her legs, doing the fastest backstroke she could manage. It felt good, pulling herself through the sea and away from the shore. She didn't stop until she was out of breath. Then she trod water.

That was odd. The campsite had another tent in it now. A big bright yellow one. No one could have put a tent up that quickly. It must have been there before. Martha didn't know how she could have missed it.

The sky looked different now, too. It was streaked with violet, which was unusual for the time of day. Violet was more of a sunset colour, Martha thought, and it wasn't even lunchtime yet. Not only that, but the violet streaks were shining, too, with a smattering of silver sparkles. Was that the reflection of the seawater? She'd never seen violet streaks and sparkles in Archwell. Maybe the sky just looked different in Wales. Either that, or she was seeing things.

Martha was surprised to see how far out she had swum. She had already drawn level with the end of the headland, and she could see the little strip of beach that Sam had said was called Nohaven. It was backed by rocks and completely deserted. It would be very private there. A place where you could be totally alone and no one would bother you and ask you what you were thinking. The cove was only a few metres away. She was just starting to swim towards it when she heard someone calling her name. She sighed as she saw Mum, Sam and Robbie, all at the water's edge, all waving their arms and yelling at her to come back.

✴ ✴ ✴

'What were you doing all the way out there?' Mum demanded when she'd made it back to the shore.

'Swimming, of course.' Martha stood up in the shallow water. 'I was going to swim to Nohaven.'

Sam made a face. 'Not a great idea. There are some really dangerous currents here. Even the best swimmers could get into trouble.'

'Yes,' agreed Robbie. 'And there could be rip tides. I've heard about them. They can pull you to your death in seconds. Rip tides are extreme, aren't they, Sam?'

Sam ruffled Robbie's hair. 'If you really want to go to Nohaven, Martha,' he said, 'best thing is to walk round at low tide. It's when the tide's on the turn you have to watch out. The water comes in at a cracking pace then. We could do that walk one day, if you like.'

'No thanks. I've gone off it now.' Martha knew she was being rude, but she didn't care. She wasn't going to do anything Sam suggested. She strode off up the beach.

'Do you know what the world record is for holding your breath underwater?'

Robbie was trotting along beside her.

'No,' said Martha, although she knew she was about to find out.

'It's nineteen minutes and twenty-one seconds. Which is amazing. Most people would run out of puff in much less time. I've tried it in the bath, and I can only do sixty-seven seconds. I wonder how long Sam can do.'

Suddenly, something caught Martha's eye further along the beach. An animal with a stubby tail disappeared inside one of Sam and Robbie's carefully constructed sand tunnels.

'You'd have to be specially trained to do it for as long as that world champion did,' Robbie carried on, 'get your lungs stretched and things. Otherwise they might collapse like one of those whoopee cushions.' He slapped his palms together and made a farting noise with his mouth. 'Just like that. The air's gone, and it's all over.'

The tunnel ran right round the castle moat. Martha paused, waiting for the animal to reappear.

'Why have we stopped?' said Robbie. 'Anyway, that guy who did the nineteen minutes is so slick. He must be like one of those creatures that can live on land or water. You know, like frogs and newts. What do you call those things?'

'Garnet?' Martha murmured, as the animal's head popped out of the tunnel.

'No, it's *amphi* something. Yeah, that's it. Amphibians! How cool would it be to be one of those?' Robbie hesitated. 'What did you say?'

'Garnet,' Martha repeated.

'What about him?'

'I saw him.'

'What? Did you? Where?'

'There. Running around your sandcastle.'

'Oh, cool! Let's go and see him.' Robbie began to run towards the castle.

Martha grabbed his arm. 'No, wait.' Garnet couldn't be here. She must be imagining it. She remembered how she had done that before when Opal had disappeared for a while. She'd wanted to see her so much that she kept on thinking she did see her. It was always really disappointing when it turned out to be someone else entirely.

'It's not Garnet,' she said firmly. 'He's in Archwell. It must be just some dog.'

They both stood staring at the animal that was pottering about on Castle Extreme, sniffing at the turrets and flags.

'It's not some dog.' Robbie pulled away. 'It's definitely him. Look, he's all spotty and stripy.'

The animal looked their way, wrinkling its small pink nose as it sniffed the air. *Chigga-chee!*

That was the sound Garnet always made, but it couldn't be him. Because if it was, Opal would be all on her own and that was something that could never happen.

'Hey, Garnie!' Robbie called as he charged off. 'How are you, boy? I missed you!'

The animal did seem to recognise Robbie. It ran towards him and jumped into his arms and licked his ears.

Martha shook her head. She knew perfectly well that Garnet would never leave Opal alone because she would die without him. No, the only way Garnet could have left Archwell and come all the way to Stormhaven was if . . . if . . .

'Ahoy there, camp-mates!'

Martha looked up.

'Surprise, surprise!' The cheery voice from above was very familiar.

Shielding her eyes from the sun, Martha saw a girl standing on the very edge of the clifftop, waving both arms at them as if she was a windmill on an exceptionally windy day. There was no mixing her up with anyone else this time. It was Opal Moonbaby, laughing and jiggling about and dressed for the beach.

She waved her sunglasses at them. 'Aren't I a sight for four eyes!' she cried.

Martha felt her heart flip right over. She couldn't have stopped it if she'd wanted to.

'Opal.' She was so stunned she could only whisper. 'You're here.'

'You bet your best bananas, I am!' Opal bellowed. 'Wait there. I'll be down in two tocks. I'm taking the short-nick!'

Opal completely ignored the path down to the beach. She swung herself round and climbed onto the cliff face, reaching her arms and legs out wide as she searched for footholds. She reminded Martha of the stretchy, sticky toys that could cling to glass and walk down windows.

'Should she be doing that?' asked Robbie, squinting up at Opal.

Martha put her hands over her eyes as she thought about how those stretchy toys sometimes stopped sticking to the windows they were walking down and fell off, landing flat on their backs.

'It's not safe to climb on the cliffs. I don't think she read the sign.' Opal never read signs, especially ones with warnings on them. She always leaped into things without thinking. That was why she needed Martha with her, to keep her safe on Earth. If she made it down to the beach in one piece, maybe Martha would still be able to do that. She might, if they were going to be friends again. Martha wasn't sure about that yet.

'Whoops-a-pansy!' Opal cried, as clumps of dry earth fell away and she lost her footing for a moment. Then she took a flying leap off the cliff face and landed in the sand like a long-jump champion, right in front of Martha, safe and sound and as bouncy as ever.

Opal stood up, her sun hat flapping gently and then settling down on her head the way a butterfly might settle on a flower. She stared at Martha intently.

Opal's violet eyes were concentrating on her with such intense energy that Martha felt as if she was being absorbed by them.

She blinked hard and looked away. Really she felt like flinging her arms round Opal and hugging her, but she didn't do that. The memory of their last meeting, and Opal's coldness towards her, held her back.

Opal didn't hesitate, though. She lunged forward, swept Martha up into her arms and spun her round so quickly that her legs started to fly out behind her.

'Put me down, Opal! Put me down!'

Opal did. 'What's up, Martha?' she said. 'You are pleased to see me, aren't you? Everything's chunky-dory, isn't it?'

'*Hunky*-dory.' Martha stepped away, pulling down the edges of her swimsuit, which had ridden up during the overenthusiastic embrace. 'And I don't know if it is or not.'

Robbie was unaware of anything except Garnet, who had rolled over in the moat of Castle Extreme and was wriggling on his back, ready to play. Robbie grabbed a feather from the tallest sand turret and tickled him with it, letting the mingle hold it in his paws and gnaw on it.

Opal hopped about, looking ready to bubble over, like a fizzy drink that has been poured too quickly.

'I'm so extra zooming sorry, Martha!' she burst out. She took Martha's hand and pulled her along the beach. 'I've wounded your feelings. I've trampled all over them and crushed them. I should never have done it.'

'Then why *did* you?' said Martha.

'I know I was horrible,' wailed Opal. 'And I'm sorry. But I can explain. I'll come squeaky clean now,

I will. I want to put all my cards out in the open.'

'OK,' said Martha. 'I'm listening.'

'I was trying to play it cold.'

'Play it cool, you mean? With me?'

'Yes,' Opal went on. 'It was a big mistake, I know that now. But I thought I could make things easier for you. You see, I saw what you were thinking when I was on that Bucking Bronco.'

'What do you mean?'

'I saw how much you didn't want to say goodbye. How painful it was going to be for you. How you'd rather die than go through with it. Remember?'

Martha nodded. She did remember thinking those things.

'Well, I thought I could save you from all that. I thought if I pretended I didn't care about going back to Carnelia and leaving you behind, well, maybe I really wouldn't care. Maybe you wouldn't care either. Then, when the time came for me to go, you might decide I wasn't worth the bother and you wouldn't mind. You wouldn't miss me so much. I only did it because I thought it was for the best. I thought it would help if I made a clean chop.'

'A clean chop,' Martha repeated. She smiled and shook her head. Suddenly she understood. Opal had been trying to make a clean break. She had been doing it for Martha's sake, to save her feelings.

'So, you do care about me really?'

'Oh, I do,' said Opal with great seriousness. 'I may be an alien but I do care. I care so much about you, Martha, that while you've been away I've been shouting your name all round Archwell. I've been howling it all over the place. Like this.'

Opal threw back her head and yowled at the blue sky. 'Ow-ow-ow-*owwwwwww*!'

Martha and Robbie put their hands over their ears until they were sure she had finished.

'And that's not all. I've been writing your name everywhere, too. I've been writing it on every piece of paper that comes my way. In fact, I can't stop writing it. Look, I'm doing it now! I can't zooming help it!'

Opal had grabbed a stick of driftwood and was carving out the letters of Martha's name in the sand. 'This is all very un-Carnelian, you know,' she said, glancing up from her work. 'Uncle Bixbite wouldn't approve of this behaviour at all.'

'Why not?' said Martha. She watched her name appear in the sand and tried not to smile. It was such a relief to see Opal back to her old, funny ways.

'It's not logical,' said Opal. 'That's why not. But I can't help it. I can't resist it. When I can't see you, Martha, I get a pain here.' She pressed her hands to her heart. 'And when I know I am going to see you I get these funny feelings in my feet, and in my hands.' She wiggled her little fingers. 'My little rosies tingle so much I start wondering if they might actually drop off! And now that I *can* see you, Martha, now that I'm with you again, I feel so happy I could . . . I could do *this*!'

Opal looked for a moment as if she was going to cry, but 'face-leaking', as she called it, was something she had never done. Instead of shedding tears, Opal threw herself on her back, stuck her feet in the air and grabbed them with her hands. She rolled around in the sand like a wildly happy greyhound that has just been let off the lead.

Martha burst out laughing. She had been missing Opal terribly; it was a big relief to know that Opal had been missing her just as much.

She pulled Opal to her feet and hugged her.

'I missed you too,' she said. 'Loads.'

'Me too,' said Robbie. 'Hey, what's Garnie doing with my pebble collection?' Garnet was picking small stones from Robbie's pebble pile and arranging them on the sand. Four letters appeared.

B B F L

Garnet sat back on his haunches and whined.

'BBFL,' Martha said. 'What's that?'

'Bonnie-Belle-Flower-Lady,' said Opal. 'Garnet's missing her now, like I missed you.'

'Oh, poor Garnie,' said Robbie, patting him. 'Don't worry. We'll look after you. And aren't you clever, knowing how to do initials?'

Garnet licked Robbie's face, which set Robbie off in a sneezing fit. Much as he loved Garnet, he was still allergic to him. The mingle sat down in the sand and wagged his tail politely, waiting for the sneezing to finish.

'So you're not angry with me any more, Martha?' said Opal. 'You don't think I'm a robot any longer?' She strutted mechanically up and down.

'No, I'm not angry,' said Martha. She looked down and noticed the edge of the postcard she had begun writing sticking out of the sand. She felt a bit embarrassed that she hadn't written it properly yet. She tried to cover the rest of it up with her toe.

'A postcard!' said Opal, her eyes lighting on it immediately. 'Is that for me? You were going to send me one after all?'

'I was,' said Martha. 'A bit later on.'

She went to pick the postcard up but Opal was quicker and snatched it out of the sand. 'Wish you were here,' she read, nodding approvingly at the picture on the front. 'Well, I am here now, so that's all right.' She turned the card over and saw the words

Dear Opal

and the yawning blank space underneath.

'It's not finished,' Martha started, but Opal was clasping the card to her heart.

'Dear Opal,' she breathed. 'Dear Opal. Oh, Martha,

that's the most wonderful thing anyone's ever said to me.' She skipped around in a circle. 'Dear Opal, dear Opal, dear Opal!'

She whooped and danced about, almost bumping into Mum and Sam as they arrived, dripping, from a swim.

'Hello, Opal,' said Mum, grabbing a towel. 'Fancy seeing you in Stormhaven! Did your uncle bring you along?'

Martha waited to hear what Opal would say. In all the excitement she had forgotten to ask her how she had got here.

'Not exactly, Marie Stephens.' Opal bowed to Mum. 'It's a bit of a tall tale, actually. It all began when—'

'*Opal Amethyst Lapis Lazuli Moonbaby!*' A majestic voice rang out over the cove. Dust and a few small rocks crumbled down from the cliff face.

'Oops, sounds like the gods are angry,' said Sam, and everyone looked up to see Uncle Bixbite standing on the cliff edge. Even from that distance it was clear he was furious. He raised a hand and beckoned Opal to him. Martha hoped he hadn't come to take her away. Opal had only just arrived.

'Sorry to interrupt myself like this,' Opal said, 'but I think I'm needed.' She leaped onto the rock face. 'See you laters, radiators!' she called.

'Not that way, Opal,' Mum cried. 'It's not safe.'

'In a while, carpet tile!' Opal sang as she started to

climb. She scaled the rock easily. Garnet scrambled after her and hitched a ride on her head.

'Neat,' murmured Sam. 'Pretty neat.'

'Hmm,' said Mum. 'Nevertheless, I think we'll take the long way round. And don't let me catch you two trying a stunt like that.'

Quickly, Martha stuffed her belongings into her bag and helped roll up the towels. She would have liked to follow Opal up the cliff face if Mum hadn't been there, and if she hadn't been afraid of heights. Now that Opal had arrived, she didn't want to let her out of her sight.

She hurried up the winding path ahead of the others, her head buzzing with questions. How had Opal got to Stormhaven in the first place? Had she travelled in the Domestipod? In broad daylight? If she had, where was it now? And why was Uncle Bixbite here? But all these questions could wait. The path was steep but Martha found herself skipping up it with energy to spare. She and Opal were friends again. Opal was here. Now they could really get this summer holiday back on track!

The campsite was just the same as when they had left it, except for one thing. A new, very large, very yellow tent had been set up slap bang in the middle of the field. Martha had spotted it from the sea. It was different from the other tents because it had no windows, and as far as Martha could tell, no door. The shiny yellow material was very familiar. Martha was pretty sure she recognised it.

'Interesting,' said Sam, coming up the path behind her. 'Must be one of those new high-tech jobs. That your friend's tent, is it?'

'Think so.' And if she was right about that material, something told Martha she didn't want Sam getting too close to this tent.

'Extreme!' Sam nodded approvingly. When she

didn't answer he said, 'Right, let's get that kettle on.' He headed off to their tent. Whatever else Martha thought about Sam, at least he seemed to know when he wasn't wanted.

Martha looked for Opal. She had disappeared, but Uncle Bixbite was there. He was deep in conversation with the farmer. She was a thin woman with short hair and big boots and she was waving her arms crossly.

'Wow!' Robbie came up, panting. 'Uncle Bixbite's actually here. The King of Carnelia is on our campsite! I can't believe it. That is so slick! Why isn't he wearing the Coronet, though?'

'How many people do you know who go round with crowns on their heads?'

'Oh, yes, see what you mean,' said Robbie. 'People might notice.'

Martha shushed him as she tried to listen to what the farmer was saying.

'You didn't phone to book,' she grumbled. 'That space could have been reserved for someone else.'

'But it wasn't reserved, was it?' said Uncle Bixbite, while the farmer's dog sniffed curiously at his shiny shoes. He'd probably never smelt an alien before.

'Well, no, not as it turns out,' said the farmer, 'but—'

'What a happy coincidence for us, then. Reverse!' Uncle Bixbite snapped his fingers at the dog, who immediately stopped sniffing, took a few steps backwards and sat down. Uncle Bixbite turned his attention back to the farmer and put on his most charming smile. Martha wondered what the farmer would say if she knew she was having a conversation with the ruler of a completely different planet.

'Yes, well,' the farmer dropped her gaze, 'the pitch is twelve pounds a night. Shower and toilet block's over there. Campfires allowed so long as you're careful. No littering, no language and no noise after ten p.m. This is a family site. OK?'

'OK, indeed,' said Uncle Bixbite, inclining his head to show that the conversation was finished.

The farmer said, 'Hmph,' and stomped back to the farmhouse. Her dog shambled after her.

Uncle Bixbite nodded to Martha and Robbie. They both bowed instinctively. They couldn't help it. Even without the Carnelian Coronet on his head, Uncle Bixbite was still every inch a king. He caught sight of Mum and Sam trying to light the gas on Sam's little camping stove, and strode over to join them.

Martha watched as Mum introduced him to Sam. Mum thought Uncle Bixbite was an astronaut living in Archwell with Opal. She must be telling Sam that because he was looking very impressed as he shook Uncle Bixbite's hand.

'What is *that*?' said Robbie, only just spotting the new arrival on the campsite, 'the world's most windowless tent?'

He went over and pinched the yellow fabric between his fingers. 'Wait a minute,' he said. 'Haven't I seen this somewhere before?'

'Yes,' said Martha. 'You have.'

'This isn't a proper tent at all, is it?' said Robbie.

'No. It's Mrs Underedge's parachute silk. Opal said she'd store it for her after the Fete, inside the Domestipod.' Martha pressed her palm against the material and her hand immediately met a flat, hard surface, like a wall. 'Only, if you ask me, she's doing it the other way around.'

'How do you mean?'

'I don't think Opal's storing the parachute silk inside the Domestipod,' said Martha. 'I think she's storing the Domestipod inside the parachute silk.'

'Had to,' said Opal, sticking her head out from underneath the parachute, her cheek resting on the dry grass. 'The Domestipod is travelling in an incognito fashion. You were all at the beach when I arrived. No one saw me. I threw Mrs U's parachute over the top as soon as I landed. Didn't want too many questions being asked.'

'Questions seem to be being asked anyway,' said Martha, thinking of the farmer. Things seemed quite calm now, though. She watched Uncle Bixbite talking to Mum, while Sam poured them all a cup of tea.

'Are you two coming in?' said Opal. 'Or are you going to stay out there until Zoomsday?' Her head disappeared.

Martha and Robbie looked at one another. Then, as there was no sign of any other available entrance, they dropped to the ground and scrambled under the parachute silk after Opal.

✸ ✸ ✸

The Domestipod really was underneath the parachute silk, looking exactly as it always did. It must have travelled extremely smoothly, because even the flowers growing around its base were completely undisturbed. Luckily it was only a very little house, so the whole thing fitted snugly inside the parachute.

Inside, everything was in its usual place. All Opal's things were there: her hammock, Garnet's hammock, the beanbags, the tongue-shaped table and the stools on springs, the shower cubicle and the scoff-capsule dispenser. Opal had brought her entire home and all her belongings to the beach. It was so funny. They could even pretend they were back in Archwell if they wanted.

There were two things that were different. The first was that everything had been covered in graffiti. Opal hadn't been kidding when she said she'd been writing Martha's name all over the place, and she hadn't restricted herself to writing it on paper, either. It was all over the walls, the table and the stools. It was even on the moon-shaped light shade.

There was also a new addition to the room. A big silvery metal cube had been pushed into the corner. It was even more noticeable now because it was the only thing Opal hadn't written on. She must have avoided it on purpose.

The cube had a flap at the top, the type you might need if you were posting an extremely large letter. Martha realised it was the object that had been covered with a cloak before, the object she had mistaken for a fridge, the object that had made Opal use her eye power against Martha for the first time ever. Now that Martha could see the whole thing, it didn't look much like a fridge after all. It had a silver cylinder sticking up on top of it, like a small clean chimney.

Martha glanced at Opal. What was this new silver cube for, and why had Opal been so keen to stop her from seeing it?

Opal didn't seem to want to answer that question. She reached up and scooped Garnet off the light shade where he was perching, and hugged him to her. Martha decided not to ask Opal out loud. She didn't want to risk being called a nosy poker again; they had only just made up. And Opal had said she was going to put all her cards on the table. The chances were she would tell her about the silver cube when she was good and ready. Martha decided to wait for that time and, as she did so, Opal gave her a grateful look.

'I resent this, Opal.' Uncle Bixbite did a very elegant forward roll through the door of the Domestipod and stood up, picking stray grass from his navy-blue suit. 'Thanks to you, I resemble an Earth pig that has rolled in the hay!'

Martha and Robbie started bowing all over again, and Martha found herself wishing she'd brushed her hair and that there wasn't a greasy mayonnaise mark on her shorts.

'No need for bowing and scraping, Earth children,' said Uncle Bixbite. 'Kindly desist, and sit down.' They sat down on the stools on springs. Martha tried not to bob about too much on hers. It didn't seem polite to bob up and down in front of the Carnelian Coronet-holder.

'You, on the other hand,' Uncle Bixbite said to Opal, 'should be on your knees, kissing my feet with gratitude. I have just wasted a valuable half-hour, pouring oil on the waters you have troubled so violently and, I may say, so unnecessarily.'

He pulled a tortoiseshell clothes brush from his jacket pocket and began to sweep it across his suit. Then he took his hand away, but the clothes brush didn't fall to the floor as Martha expected it to. It stayed where it was and kept brushing.

It wasn't a brush; it was a tortoise, or perhaps a terrapin, with a million hairy white feet underneath its shell. They were marching about like a small army of millipedes.

'That's his mingle,' Robbie whispered. 'Must be.'

Martha frowned. The creature did look like a mingle. That's what a mingle was, after all – a mix of several different animals. The clothes brush was eyeing her with one beady squirrel eye that looked much too big for the side of its small terrapin head. It was definitely a mingle of some sort, but as Martha watched it trekking slowly across Uncle Bixbite's shoulders, something about it bothered her.

She remembered Uncle Bixbite's mingle from before, and it hadn't looked like this. It had been mainly bat, with eagle eyes and the feathers of an exotic bird. Where was that mingle now, and why did Uncle Bixbite have this new one? Maybe if you were the ruler of the whole planet you were allowed to have more than one. That was the only explanation Martha could think of.

'Opal,' Uncle Bixbite said severely. 'What do you mean by flying around Earth in broad daylight, after all that I've told you? Your time on this planet is very nearly up. Soon you will return to Carnelia and claim your CIA. I will admit,' he cleared his throat, 'that following a somewhat rocky beginning, you have had a highly successful year. Now the Carnelians await your return. *I* await your return. It is almost time for you to apply your mind to Matters of Planet. Remember, Opal, soon it will be you, not I, who wears the Carnelian Coronet.'

'Wow!' Robbie hissed in Martha's ear. 'Opal's going to be Queen of Carnelia! How extreme is *that*!'

Martha nudged him to shut him up.

'I grow weary, Opal,' Uncle Bixbite said, and he did look tired. His blue eyes were as sharp and piercing as ever but his pale face was even paler than usual and there were lines on his forehead that looked as if someone had drawn them there with thick pencil.

'I find I am looking forward to my retirement, and to handing you the reins of Carnelia. However,' he pulled himself up to his full height, 'I shall never be able to do so if you insist on gallivanting around the Earth's atmosphere and risk giving away your true identity. If word gets out that you are from another planet, you will never even be awarded the Carnelian Independence Award, let alone be permitted to inherit the Coronet.

'I am flabbergasted!' Uncle Bixbite continued. 'Why would you choose to jeopardise your future? My future? The very future of Carnelia? You moved the Domestipod in a foolhardy manner. Logic is king, Opal. That is the first rule of Carnelia. And yet your behaviour today crosses the very bounds of reason. How do you explain it?'

Martha had no idea how Opal was going to answer such a severe and solemn speech. She wouldn't like to be in her shoes now. Mum told her off sometimes, but Mum wasn't half as scary as this. Opal didn't seem afraid though, not a bit.

She shrugged and said simply, 'I wanted to be with Martha. I couldn't stay away from her. I tried, but I couldn't because her absence made my heart grow tender.'

Even though she was afraid of Uncle Bixbite's anger, Martha couldn't hide a smile. Opal's words made her feel warm all the way through.

The silence that followed was long and alarming. Opal and her uncle stared at one another. Opal returned Uncle Bixbite's clear blue gaze with her own bright violet one. Neither of them blinked for what seemed like minutes.

Garnet crept onto Robbie's knee and Robbie sneezed violently, making Martha jump, but Opal didn't bat an eyelid, and nor did Uncle Bixbite. They just kept staring at each other while Uncle Bixbite's mingle progressed slowly down one of his jacket sleeves, removing specks of dust.

It was Uncle Bixbite who at last broke the silence. 'Are you trying to tell me, niece,' he said, raising his eyebrows, 'that human beings are made of some magnetic substance? Is that what you would have me believe?'

'Do you know, I think they must be!' said Opal, jumping sideways towards Martha and taking her hand. 'This one must be, anyway. I'm drawn to Martha like metal to a magnet. Like a mop to a flame. I want to be close to her all the time. I don't know why it's like that, Uncle Bixie, but it is.'

Martha felt so pleased to hear Opal talk about her in this way, but very embarrassed that Uncle Bixbite had to be there hearing it too. The lines on his forehead were growing even deeper and darker.

'If I didn't know better, Opal,' he said, 'I would say you were starting to indulge in the worst kind of human behaviour. Illogical behaviour. *Emotional* behaviour.' He said the word 'emotional' as if it had a sour taste, as if he'd just been made to lick a lemon. 'This is the type of behaviour you have been recording in the *Human Handybook*. Behaviour that belongs on Earth, and not on Carnelia. It is most certainly not appropriate behaviour for the heir to the Carnelian Coronet.'

He moved closer, towering over Martha and Opal. 'I see now,' he boomed, 'that your return to Carnelia is long overdue. The ways of this little world are rubbing off on you in a dangerous manner. The sooner you come home, the better.'

Martha gripped Opal's hand in panic. She was terribly afraid Uncle Bixbite would wrench Opal away right now, and that they would lose their last precious days together after all.

'I can't come now, Uncle.' Opal squeezed Martha's hand. 'I have to stay until the twenty-sixth of August, or I won't fulfil the challenge.'

'I realise that.' Uncle Bixbite plucked the clothes-brush mingle from his suit and paced about the room. 'But there must be no more revelations to

Earth dwellers, and no more risk-taking. Do you understand me?'

'I understand, Uncle Bixie,' said Opal cheerfully. 'I understand very well. You want me to shake up and smell the toffee!'

'Not how I would have put it,' said Uncle Bixbite, still pacing. 'But I want you to remember that logic is everything. Logic is king. If you remember that, then all should be well.' He put his new mingle away in his pocket. 'Now, I must be getting back. Unfortunately Carnelia does not run itself when I am absent.'

He stopped then, seeing the silver cube in the corner of the room.

'Ah,' he said, 'I was beginning to wonder if this had not arrived. I thought it ought to be here, since I sent it by special cosmic courier. Now, Opal, why on Carnelia haven't you used it yet?'

Opal suddenly dropped Martha's hand into her lap. For the first time during the interview with Uncle Bixbite, she looked uncomfortable. Whatever the silver cube was, it was clear that Opal found even the smallest mention of it upsetting.

'I will use it,' she said. 'Of course I will. I'm just waiting for the . . . for the right time.'

'There's no *time* like the present!' Uncle Bixbite patted the cube. 'Make sure it is done, Opal, and quickly. There can be no reason for delay.' He glared at Opal and then at Garnet, who was rattling his cat biscuits as he arranged them in the initials of Bonnie-Belle-Flower-Lady's name.

Martha guessed that Uncle Bixbite didn't like being interrupted, especially by a mingle. That must be why he was giving Garnet such a hard stare.

'I shall return to my spaceship,' he said. 'I have secreted it behind the shower block, and need to be off before the farmer does her evening rounds. I shall make my own way; there is no need to escort me.'

He bowed briefly to Martha and Robbie, who both got up and bowed back. 'Farewell, young Earthlings,' he said.

He turned to Opal who was bending over Garnet, fondling the wispy lynx hairs on the tops of his pointed ears. 'Farewell, Opal. I will return just once more on the twenty-sixth of this planet's August. I shall look forward to receiving your Full and Final Earth Report on that date. Then you will make your Final Ascendance and commence your Carnelian Ruler's Apprenticeship. Until then, remember what I have told you.'

'Yes, Uncle,' said Opal. 'I know. Twenty-sixth of August. Full and Final Report. Logic is king.' She was smiling, but her voice sounded softer than usual, almost sad.

Uncle Bixbite straightened his back. Opal stood to attention. Moving in unison, like mirror images of one another, they each held up one hand and crossed it with the palm of the other. That, Martha now knew, was the Carnelian salute.

'*Vatengpaxxz*,' they said together.

Then Uncle Bixbite marched out of the Domestipod door. He dropped smoothly to the ground and lifted the parachute silk. Stopping just long enough to give Opal one last meaningful stare, he slid under it and rolled neatly away.

'*Vatengpaxxz!*' Robbie said, trying to imitate Uncle Bixbite's deep voice. '*Vatengpaxxz, Vatengpaxxz!*' He strutted around the Domestipod, giggling.

Martha started giggling too. Even Opal chuckled.

Once she started laughing, Martha found she couldn't stop. She wasn't laughing because of Robbie, really, but because Uncle Bixbite had gone. Opal's uncle was a wonderful person but he could be very intense, and it was a relief when he went away.

'Hang on a minute,' said Robbie, once they'd stopped laughing. 'Let's make sure he's really gone.'

They put their heads out of the parachute silk just in time to see what looked like a navy-blue arrow

6

shooting silently through the sky. It disappeared into the clouds, leaving a shimmer of blue and silver light.

'Extreme!' Robbie marvelled. 'That thing must be travelling at the speed of sound. Maybe even the speed of light! It's got to be a world record!'

'Universe record, more like,' said Opal. 'Carnelian spaceships make your Earth rockets look like old tortoises on their holidays.'

Martha kept looking at the unnaturally blue sky. 'The sky was all pinky-mauve earlier, and a bit starry. Was that you, Opal? In the Domestipod?'

'Certainly was. Our spaceships fly so fast, the human eye can only see the light vapours they leave behind. Just as well, really. Flying houses are one-a-penny-farthing on Carnelia, but they're quite rare on your planet. They'd attract a bit too much attention.'

'That's so extreme!' Robbie said again.

'Do you have to keep saying that word?' Martha said. 'It's really irritating.'

'Why shouldn't I say it? I like it. Sam says it all the time.'

That's just the point, Martha thought, but she didn't say so.

Robbie turned to Opal. 'Hey, do you think we could show Sam round the Domestipod one day? He loves cars and planes and motorboats and stuff. He's always watching *Rev It Up!* on TV.'

Robbie laced his fingers together and stretched out his hands. Martha knew he was remembering their own trip in the Domestipod, when they had flown with Opal to the island of Muckle Flugga. It had been wonderful, like being caught up in a fabulous whirlwind. Neither of them would ever forget it.

'Aw, I wish we could take Sam for a flight in your house, Opal!'

'Don't be an idiot!' said Martha. 'You mustn't ever tell Sam anything about it. He might go to the newspapers, or put it on the Internet. He could ruin Opal's chances of getting her CIA.'

'Sam wouldn't do that,' said Robbie. 'Sam's great.'

'You don't know what he might do.' Martha insisted. 'You have to keep quiet!' It wasn't only the CIA Martha was worried about. The truth was, she didn't want to share Opal with anyone new at this stage, least of all Sam. She gave Robbie a sharp prod in the back to emphasise her point. She couldn't say any more because Mum and Sam were on their way over.

Mum was smiling. 'So, Martha,' she said, 'looks like you can spend the holiday with your friend after all.'

'Oh, thank you, Marie Stephens,' said Opal, bouncing up and down. 'Thank you for agreeing to keep an ear on me while I'm camping.'

'That's OK,' said Mum. 'Your uncle has explained why he can't stay.'

'Has he?' said Martha. 'Really?' For a moment she thought Uncle Bixbite might have let Mum in on the whole secret, but Mum wouldn't have been looking so matter-of-fact about everything if that was true, would she?

'Yes, he's told me all about the difficult mission he's on. Sounds terribly important. I wouldn't want to stand in the way of an astronaut's work. In any case, I don't think you three are going to need much looking after. This is a very safe place for children, as long as you don't stray too far. And as long as you don't go near the cliffs.' She gave Opal a long look. 'Then I'll hardly need to watch you at all.'

'Woohoo! Freedom at last!' yelled Robbie.

'Anyone want to go crabbing at the harbour before supper?' said Sam. 'I've got a bit of bacon and some crab lines.'

'No thanks,' Martha replied. 'We're busy.'

'Are we?' asked Opal.

'No we're not,' said Robbie.

'Yes,' Martha said. 'Sorry, but we are.' She liked the idea of crabbing, but she was watching the farmer's dog sniffing round the Domestipod, sticking its nose under the parachute silk. The first thing they needed to do was make sure the silk was firmly pegged down.

Mum said, 'I think Martha would like to move her sleeping bag over to Opal's tent now, wouldn't you, love?'

'Yes, please!' It wasn't what Martha had been thinking, but there was nothing she wanted more. Now she could be with Opal twenty-four hours a day.

'Yesss!' Opal cried. 'We can be tent-mates!'

'And me,' said Robbie. 'I want to come too!'

'Not you,' Mum said. 'Let the girls be on their own for a bit.'

'What?' Robbie looked ready to argue.

'Oh no, we can't spare you, Robbie,' Sam said. 'If you go over there, who's going to read the *Guinness Book of World Records* to me at night? I'll never get to sleep without that!'

Robbie gave Sam a push, but he wasn't really cross. He loved reading facts out of his record book.

Sam grinned at Martha. 'Means you can have a break from your brother's footballs too, doesn't it? Don't suppose they make very comfy pillows. Do you want a hand with your stuff?'

'No,' Martha said quickly. 'No thanks. We can manage.' She wasn't being deliberately mean to Sam, but the last thing she wanted was for him and Mum to see the Domestipod. They'd recognise it immediately and want to know how it had got here from Archwell. Martha wouldn't be able to explain that away in a hurry.

'*I'll* come to the harbour and catch crabs with you, Sam,' said Mum. 'Wouldn't want you to be lonely.' She took his hand and they wandered away together.

'They've gone all lovey-dovey again,' said Robbie.

'Lovey-dovey?' said Opal. She flickered her eyes, looking the term up in her brain dictionary. '*Lovey-*

111

dovey,' she read from her mind. '*Expressing affection in an extravagantly sentimental way; mushy.* Oh, I get it! When humans really like each other, they behave like squashy peas!'

'*Seriously* squashy peas,' said Martha, wrinkling her nose, but she didn't mind all that much, not now that Opal was here.

Opal grinned. 'I'm so glad I came, Martha!' she said. 'Now I can spend the rest of my Earth summer with you. It's all I want. I'm so deliriously, blissfully ecstatic. Do you know, I feel a bit like a squashy pea myself!' She gave Martha a big squeeze.

Martha laughed and squeezed her back. 'Me too!' she said.

'Gross!' said Robbie. 'You're it, by the way!' He touched Opal on the arm, jumped over the guy ropes of a nearby tent and ran away to the clifftop. Opal ran after him, while Garnet circled them both, leaping at their knees.

Martha went to look in Sam's cool box and pulled out some spoons Mum was keeping in there. She didn't think she'd miss just a few. She shooed the dog away from the Domestipod and then went round slotting the spoon handles through the eyelets in the parachute silk, pressing them deep into the ground until she was satisfied that Opal's home was secure inside. Or as secure as it possibly could be in the middle of a campsite.

'Woohoo!' Opal cried, lolloping about, still trying

to tag Robbie. 'Come back here, you slippery fishcake!'

Robbie laughed and nipped away, dodging her outstretched hand.

Opal giggled and whooped. 'Come on, Martha,' she called. Garnet seemed to be tiring a little, so she scooped him up and tucked him gently under her armpit. 'Garnet and I need your help! We're a pair of damsons in distress!'

Opal didn't look as if she was in distress. She didn't look as if she had any secrets either, or a care in the world. But after seeing her with Uncle Bixbite, Martha felt sure something was troubling her friend. The silver cube inside the Domestipod was a mystery. She hoped Opal would tell her what the problem was soon; then she'd be able to help her with it.

For now, though, the sky was blue and clear; there was barely a breeze to ruffle the long grass or the pink and white clover heads that dotted the field. Opal still had fourteen days left on Earth, and she was going to spend every one of them with Martha.

At this precise moment, there was only one thing Martha wanted to do. She skipped away from the Domestipod and broke into a run.

'Look out for me, you two!' she yelled as she raced across the field. 'You don't know it yet, but I'm the champion tagger of Stormhaven!'

'Come on, Opal!' Robbie shouted. 'The water's lovely this morning. Hurry up and get in!'

Opal was prancing about on the damp sand in her swimsuit. Her sun hat flapped on her head.

'What are you waiting for?' Martha called. She and Robbie had been dying to go in the sea with Opal. This was her first morning in Stormhaven, and their first proper chance to spend time at the beach with her.

'Keep your hats on, Earth dwellers, I'm coming.' Opal waggled her big toe, poised to dip it in the sea, but a tiny wave swooshed up the beach and she ran away from it.

'It's alive!' she shrieked. 'It's after me!'

She came back to the water's edge, but each time

she did so another wave came and seemed to chase her back up the beach.

'Why won't it stand still for a second, while I get in?' she said, finally paddling in a centimetre of frothy white water. 'It's very rude!'

Martha was wondering how to reassure Opal, how to explain about tides and the moon, when Sam came sauntering across the sand, his surfboard under his arm.

Garnet jumped around his legs, play-snarling at him. *Cha-chaarrgh, cha-chaaarrggghhhh!*

Sam laughed. 'You don't scare me, Garnet.' He reached down and scratched the mingle's muzzle. 'You all right there, Opal?' he said. 'You not going in?'

'I'm not much of a swimmer, actually, Sam the Man,' Opal said.

'I could show you a few strokes, if you like,' Sam offered.

Opal clapped her hands. 'How very zooming kind of you! I'd love that.'

'In we go, then.' Sam walked into the sea.

Opal didn't follow him. 'I think I'd rather have my lesson out here, if you don't mind. I'm more of a dry land sort of girl.'

Sam paused. 'All right. I guess we can start that way, if you're worried.'

He showed Opal the arm actions for front crawl and breaststroke and butterfly. Then he got her to lie on his surfboard on the sand and showed her how to kick her legs like a frog.

After a while, Sam suggested they put it all into practice, and he walked towards the sea again. Martha could tell he was expecting Opal to follow him, but she suddenly took off on the surfboard, scooting across the sand, wheeling her arms and kicking her legs like mad. She propelled herself along with her toes and then flipped over and came back at speed, doing a very unusual form of land backstroke. She made surprisingly quick progress like that.

Martha and Robbie swam along parallel to the beach and tried to race her, but Opal was already much faster than they were. Sand showered up in all directions as she ploughed through it, backwards and forwards. Garnet rode along on top of her like a bobsleigh rider, jumping up in the air each time she flipped over. As she turned, Opal punched the air with her fist and yelled, 'Rock 'n' rule! Rock 'n' rule!'

At last, after about twenty widths of the beach, she stopped at Sam's feet.

'Thanks for teaching me to swim, Sam the Man,' she said. 'I absolutely love it! Got any more tips for me?'

'Actually,' said Sam, slowly shaking his head, 'no. I don't think there's anything more I can teach you, Opal. That was amazing!' He picked up his surfboard. 'Think I'll go and see how Marie's getting on with the crossword.'

Opal shook herself like a dog, and sand sprayed out in all directions.

'I knew I'd like it by the sea,' she said as Martha and Robbie waded out of the water. 'I knew I'd love life on the ocean rave! Let's go rock-pooling. Let's build a sand palace. Bury me up to my neck in sand, you two. Come on, turn me into one of those hairy water-girls, the ones with the long tails.' Opal threw herself down and waggled her legs expectantly at Robbie and Martha.

Opal may not have wanted to go in the water, but being at the seaside with her was still double the fun. After Martha and Robbie had finished making her into a mermaid, she had kicked her way out of her tail and begun digging vigorously. The sandcastles she built were strange. They weren't mounded like normal castles; they were low, triangular structures with very smooth surfaces. She didn't put flags on them, but carved out eye shapes on their flat roofs instead. Martha guessed they were copies of Moonbaby palaces. As soon as she finished building one, Opal kicked it apart and rushed away to build another.

Even Sam's endless foraging and rock-pooling expeditions were fun when Opal was involved. She hopped around on the edge of the rock pools, and whenever Martha plucked out a crab shell or a bit of seaweed or netted a tiny fish, Opal would whoop with delight. It made Martha feel like a brilliant magician pulling white rabbits and doves out of a black top hat.

Opal wanted to play every beach game imaginable. They played beach cricket and catch, and Piggy-in-the-Middle; they made sand sculptures and pebble towers and seaweed cities. They played beach bowls using water bottles as skittles, made up sand dances, had skipping, hopping and jumping races, and they flew Robbie's kite backwards and forwards over the beach a hundred times.

When Mum finally said they had to leave and they set off up the path to the campsite, Opal had looked back longingly at the beach. The enormous grids they had scratched out for games of hopscotch and noughts and crosses stretched right across the sand. The tide was coming in and the sea was already nibbling at the grids and starting to wash them away like a giant rubber. Opal was disappointed but Martha told her not to mind; the sea was just tidying up for them and they would be back to do it all again the next day.

☆ ☆ ☆

They had supper outside, and now Sam was building a campfire. They were going to stay up until it was dark and watch the stars.

Martha and Opal were in charge of the washing-up. Martha waited with the tea towel while Opal whooshed their dirty plates around in the washing-up bowl. Garnet sat on Opal's head, washing his tummy.

Sam was blowing on the fire, his cheeks quite red with the effort of trying to get it going. Martha noticed Opal flash her eyes in his direction, and a cluster of violet sparks rushed up to the fire and swam into it like a shoal of fish. At once the flames flared up and Sam stood back, pleased, assuming that he had started the fire just with his own lungs.

Martha took a plate from Opal and stacked it with the others. 'Using your eye power?' she said quietly.

'I know it's cheating,' said Opal, 'but I thought Sam the Man could do with a helping handful of heat. I think he deserves it, don't you? He's really making this holiday go with a fling!'

Martha shrugged. 'I suppose,' she said. She had to admit that Sam was working very hard to make sure they had fun, making campfires and teaching them to surf and to dive, helping fly kites. She didn't really want to talk about Sam, though, or think about him. She'd done plenty of that already. She only wanted to think about Opal.

'You will be careful about using your eye power, won't you, Opal? You don't want to waste it. You've got to fly the Domestipod back to Archwell yet, and all the way up to Carnelia.' Flying the Domestipod used up an awful lot of eye power, and if Opal ran it down too far she would need to go all the way to the lighthouse on Muckle Flugga for a recharge.

'Don't worry,' said Opal. 'It was only a thimbleful of eye energy. But thank you for the reminder, Martha. You're always looking out for me. You're my guardian angel, you are. You're my guiding knight.'

'Guiding *light*, I think you mean.'

'Light or knight,' said Opal. 'Whichever it is, you're always there for me.'

Martha smiled. 'I'm always there nagging you, you mean.'

'Not at all. You're just a very responsible person.' Opal waggled a plate, letting the soapy water drip off it. 'And you're my Best Friend in the Universe.'

She held the plate out. Martha took it but Opal didn't let go. She just stood there, gripping her side of the plate and staring at Martha.

'What?' Martha said. 'Have I got baked beans on my nose?'

Opal shook her head. She opened her mouth but she didn't seem to know where to begin, which was unusual for her. Normally she just launched in with the first thing on her mind.

'Do you think best friends can have secrets from each other and still be best friends?' she blurted out, suddenly letting go of the plate. 'Because I think that.'

Martha knew at once that Opal wasn't talking about just any best friends, she was talking about them. 'I don't know,' she said slowly. 'I think true best friends should be able to tell each other everything, shouldn't they?'

'I was afraid you'd say that.' Opal looked worried. 'And you're absolutely sure that's true? What if there were extra-special circumstances?'

'I don't know what extra-special circumstances there could be,' Martha said. 'I can't think of any.'

When Opal didn't respond she said gently, 'I wouldn't hide anything from you, Opal, and even if I wanted to keep something secret you'd find it out straight away. You'd see it in my mind.'

'Not necessarily,' Opal said. 'I can be quite polite now. If you had a secret that was sternly confidential and for your brain cells only, I wouldn't even look at it.'

Martha shrugged. 'Well, I don't have any secrets. There's nothing I'd keep from you, Opal.' She turned to face her. 'You can have a free pass into my mind and look at anything you like there. Go on, look. You won't find a single secret.'

'No,' said Opal, studying her seriously. 'You're right. You're not keeping any secrets. Not on purpose, anyway. The only secret in there, Martha, is the one you're keeping from yourself.'

'Don't be daft!' Martha frowned. 'How could I have a secret from myself? That's impossible.'

She looked away and stared into the fire, which was crackling nicely now. 'Anyway,' she said after a while, 'you're the one keeping a secret, Opal. Not me. Why won't you tell me what it is? I might be able to help, you know. Please tell me.'

There was a long pause. And then a big sigh.

'I want to!' Opal cried. 'I do, really I do! But I just don't think I can!' She seemed genuinely upset, and began combing Garnet's fur with her fingers as if to hide her consternation.

'Why not?' said Martha. 'Don't you trust me?'

'Oh, I do trust you, Martha. I trust you absolutely. That's just it. I trust you too much!'

Martha was baffled. 'How can you trust someone too much? That doesn't make any sense.'

'Doesn't it?'

They fell silent as a bird flew low over their heads. The thrum of its wings was strong, but it passed and faded almost at once.

Martha picked some sand out of her toenails. She could see from the way Opal was concentrating on Garnet's whiskers, stroking them one by one, that whatever was on her mind was very upsetting. Martha desperately wanted to know what it was. She wished Opal would tell her.

'All right, girls?' Sam said, coming over and picking up his drink. 'The fire's going well now, but where have Robbie and Marie got to, eh? Weren't they supposed to be looking for marshmallow sticks?' When neither of them answered he said, 'Watch the fire then, you two. I'll go and look for them.'

They were on their own. The fire snapped and fizzed. It was starting to get dark.

Suddenly Opal sprang up and started to pace round the campfire.

'There is something I haven't told you, Martha,' she said, 'and I know you know that. There's something on my brain, and it's been there for a while. I want to tell you what it is, or at least, half of me does. The other half is worried that if I tell you, we might not agree on what to do about it. You might have one idea and I might have another. And that could split us in two like a coco-fruit.' She raised an imaginary axe above her head and brought it down in front of her, making swishing and slicing sounds through her teeth.

Martha sat up. 'But Opal, I might be able to help. Whatever this secret is, it's obviously worrying you and you ought to let someone else in on it. A problem shared is a problem halved. That's what Mum always says.'

'Is it?' Opal didn't seem convinced. 'It could be a problem multiplied. My problem would become your problem too, and then it would become Robbie's problem and it would go on getting bigger and bigger and more out of control. I don't want that. I know I'm not being logical, but we've got such a short time left, I don't want anything to spoil it. And the thing is,' she stroked Garnet's fur in the wrong direction, the way he liked, 'it might not even happen, and then we would all have worried about it for nothing, wouldn't we?'

Martha sighed. This was a very difficult conversation. *What* might not happen? She didn't even know what they were talking about, except that it was almost certainly connected with the silver cube that sat in the corner of the Domestipod.

'Please don't think about that!' Opal said urgently. 'Let's just pretend that cube and this stupid secret don't even exist. Can you do that, Martha? Can you stop trying to puzzle it all together? Can you? For me?'

Martha looked into Opal's wide violet eyes as they pleaded with her. She hated seeing Opal so anxious.

'All right,' she said. 'If you're sure that's what you want. I'll try.'

Opal clutched Martha's fingers, all the while keeping a hand on Garnet. 'Thank you, Martha. You're my true friend. And please don't worry about the secret. I . . . I bet it will all come out in the washing-up!'

'Here we are, then!' Mum dropped a bundle of long sticks on the ground. She opened a big packet of marshmallows.

'Oh, goody gum-pops!' said Opal, taking a stick. She put one hand on her hip, whisked the stick through the air and pointed it at Martha. 'On your fire-guard!' she said, knitting her eyebrows together, pretending to be fierce.

'It's not for fighting with,' said Martha with a laugh. 'It's not a weapon.'

'I've got the longest one in the world,' said Robbie, appearing from the hedgerow, dragging what looked like a small tree behind him. 'It's a record-breaker!'

'A record-breaking *what*?' Opal demanded. She waggled her stick. 'What *is* it?'

'It's a toasting fork,' said Martha. 'We're using them to toast these.' She fixed a pink marshmallow on the end of Opal's stick and a white one on her own. 'Like this.' She showed Opal how to hold the marshmallow close to the flame until it began to blacken and change shape. Robbie put five marshmallows on the thinner branches of his tree and walked back to hold up its trunk. 'Tell me when mine are done,' he said. 'I can't see too well from back here.'

'Bumping belly beads!' said Opal as she tasted the first hot, gooey marshmallow. 'I never would have guessed that's what we were going to do!' She whispered to Martha, 'I'll put it straight in the *Human Handybook*. Wait till they hear about this on Carnelia. Burning sweets before you eat them. On sticks! On purpose! They'll never believe it!'

Martha watched as Opal fished her *Human Handybook* out of her shorts and wrote about marshmallow-toasting at the very bottom of the very last page. Everything that Carnelians would ever know about humans and their way of life was in that book. Martha had helped compile it. She felt proud to be the one to inform Carnelians about toasting marshmallows.

Opal stuffed the book away in her shorts and set about toasting a second marshmallow, which she fed to Garnet, taking great care not to burn his mouth. 'Get your little lamb chops round that, Garnie,' she whispered to him.

Martha had noticed Opal becoming more and more protective of Garnet recently. She'd never been like that before, not when they had first met. She used to get quite impatient with him and say, 'Darn it, Garnet!' and move him out of her way, but she didn't do that any longer. She kept him on her lap or her shoulder or her head nearly all the time. Maybe the secret had something to do with Garnet, too. Martha stopped. She realised her brain was back to doing detective work. She'd promised not to do that, and she had no intention of breaking that promise.

She looked up at the sky and tried to put it out of her mind. The stars were coming out. Sam was looking up, too. 'Let's find the constellations,' he said.

Martha was glad of the distraction. Looking for stars would take her mind off Opal's secret, whatever it was.

'There's Orion,' she said, pleased to have spotted it so quickly. Orion was the only constellation she knew.

'Good spot!' said Sam. 'You can see his belt really clearly.'

'And isn't that the Plough?' Mum said, putting an arm round Sam. 'The one that looks like a milk pan.'

'That's it. Now, if we follow the line of that pan handle, we should be able to see the Little Bear. Anyone make it out?'

'I can see the Star Sisters,' said Opal, popping a last marshmallow into her mouth.

'Star Sisters?' Sam said. 'Don't know that one.'

'Oh, that's one of the best. The Star Sisters stand together, like this.' Opal linked her arm through Martha's. 'Where one sister looks the other sister looks, when one sister shines and twinkles, so does the other. The Star Sisters are joined for all eternity. They're different but they can never be parted.' She pressed Martha's arm in hers. 'The Star Sisters are joined together forever, come Hell's bells or high waters!'

'Wow!' said Sam, craning his neck to see more of the sky. 'Those two sound pretty extreme.'

'*Well* extreme!' Robbie called from his tree-trunk post.

'Did you make them up?' Martha whispered.

''Course not,' Opal said. 'The Star Sisters are as real as you and I are, Martha. And they'll never fade.'

Martha wished she and Opal could really be like the Star Sisters. She wished *they* could never be parted. This last summer with Opal wasn't turning out as she had planned – not at all – but it was truly amazing. She decided not to worry about planning it any more. From now on she would be like Opal was, like Opal wanted her to be. She wouldn't worry about Opal's secret, whatever it was. Instead, she would make the most of every moment they had left. She would live each moment as it came.

Martha yawned lazily. It was lovely waking up each morning in the Domestipod, lying out in the hammock next to Opal's with only the moon-and-stars light shade to separate them. Mum had let her spend every night there, but she thought they were snuggled down on the ground in a tent, not suspended in the air inside Opal's purple house.

She stretched and examined the freckles on her arms. The sun had been bringing more and more out on her skin each day. They were due to go back to Archwell the next morning, and now there were too many freckles to count and only seven days left with Opal. It had been the fastest two weeks Martha had ever known. She wished she could make time stand still, so that Opal would never have to go back

to Carnelia and they could stay like this forever.

She turned over and saw Garnet sitting on the silver cube below her, washing his wings. He licked methodically at them, his tongue making an odd little rasping noise as he worked.

'Hi, Garnie,' Martha whispered so as not to disturb Opal, who was still snoring.

Garnet stopped washing and looked up at her.

Chi-wee-chi.

His voice sounded huskier than usual, as if he needed to clear his throat.

'You OK?' Martha said to him.

Garnet blinked at her. He rubbed his back against the silver cube's chimney, then resumed his slow and careful licking.

Opal let out an extra-large snore and woke herself up. As soon as she opened her violet eyes, the scoff-capsule dispenser began to hum. She smiled over at Martha.

'Morning, Best Friend in the Universe,' she said. 'Time to break our fasts, I think.'

A fountain of warm popcorn flew up to the ceiling and landed in the hammocks.

They ate it slowly, savouring the sweet taste, savouring the last of their time in Stormhaven.

Tarat-tarat!

Martha paused, a piece of popcorn held to her lips.

Tarat-tarat-tarat-tat-tat!

132

She relaxed as she recognised Robbie's special morning knock, and put the popcorn in her mouth.

Opal opened the door with a wink and Robbie rushed in, just in time to catch a second popcorn shower. He dashed around the Domestipod, holding out his t-shirt and catching popcorn in it. 'Oh, yes!' he cried, when the shirt was filled to overflowing. 'And Robbie Stephens takes the world record for maximum popcorn-catching.'

He jumped onto the silver cube next to Garnet, hugged him and began eating. 'I wiff I could get a world wecord for fumfing,' he said, his mouth stuffed full. 'It'd be fo cool!' He sneezed violently as Garnet sniffed at his t-shirt.

'*Baaatchooo!*' The sneeze was so loud and so forceful that Garnet nearly fell off the cube.

'Good grievous!' said Opal, patting her ears. 'You'll sneeze us all to Jupiter!'

'Maybe you could win the record for the world's loudest sneeze,' Martha suggested.

'Doubt it,' said Robbie. 'There's a man in China who's got that. He can sneeze at a hundred and seventy-six decibels, and that's louder than a gunshot if you want to know.'

He sat on the edge of the silver cube and swung his legs, letting his feet push the metal flap open and shut. 'What's this for, Opal? Is it a Carnelian dustbin?'

'No, it is not!' Opal swung herself down from her hammock and plucked Garnet off the silver cube.

She patted him all over, not in a petting kind of way; it was more as if she was examining him. Martha wondered if Opal thought he had fleas. She didn't know if mingles could get fleas.

Opal didn't seem to find anything. She stopped patting and said, 'Come on, Earth dwellers, let's not waste another nanosecond. Let's join Marie Stephens and Sam the Man for a second yummy fast-breaker. Then it's high old tide for the beach!'

✷ ✷ ✷

'What shall we play first?' Opal said, skipping down the path. 'Do you want to play beach cricket, beach bowling, beach football, beach tennis, beach volleyball or bounders?'

'Not bounders!' Robbie exclaimed. 'Rounders!'

'Rounders it is,' said Opal, picking up the bat. 'Boxie I bat!'

'Bagsie I bowl,' laughed Martha.

'I'll be backstop,' said Robbie, tickling Garnet with a big gull's feather he'd found on the path.

'Who's going to field, though?' said Martha.

'Garnet will,' said Opal. 'He loves chasing things.'

'He'll never cover a pitch this size all by himself,' said Sam, coming up. 'I'll give the little chap a hand, shall I?' He jogged off and started laying out jumpers for the posts. 'Come on, Marie, you too – we could do with another pair of hands out here.'

Mum had her nose in a book. 'I'm sure you've

'got it covered,' she said with a smile. She carried on reading.

'Why does Sam always want to join in with everything we do?' Martha said it to herself as much as to Opal. She wasn't angry about it; it was useful to have him on the team, but most adults wouldn't have been so keen to play their games with them. 'He's a bit of a big kid, really, isn't he?'

'I think it's nice that he wants to join in.' Opal took a practice swing with the rounders bat. 'Carnelian adults aren't allowed to play games. They have to be stiff and serious all the livelong day. I'm sure it's not good for their health levels. When I'm Coronet-holder, I'm going to bring back games for grown-ups. In fact, I'm going to make them compulsory. No one will be allowed to go to work until they've played at least three games of Hide and Seek and six rounds of Eye-Spot.'

She held out the bat. 'Now, bowl the ball, will you, Martha? I'm going to whack this one to Waggersley, wherever that is!'

Martha bowled. Opal swung hard, missed completely and spun round and round on the spot.

'All the same,' said Martha, checking Sam was out of earshot, 'I don't always want Sam to play with us. Not all the time.'

'That's only because you're worried he's going to come and live in your flat with you,' said Opal.

'What?' spluttered Martha. She'd never said that.

Where had Opal got that idea from?

Opal looked up. 'Yes, I'm sorry to break it to you out of the bluebottle like this, Martha, but that's your secret, you see, the one you've been keeping from yourself. I'd been meaning to tell you what it was.'

'I'm not—' Martha shut her mouth, biting back words. She had been going to say it wasn't true, she couldn't care less whether Sam came to live with them or not. But now that Opal had said it, she realised that was exactly what had been worrying her for some time. Sam wasn't so bad. She'd even grown to like him on the holiday, but she was very worried about the idea of him coming to live with them.

'That's funny, Martha,' said Robbie, as he waited for her to bowl the ball, 'because I've been secretly hoping Sam *does* move in with us.'

'That's hardly a secret,' Martha replied.

'It would be so extremely extreme, though, wouldn't it, if he did!'

'Extremely awkward, more like,' said Martha. 'There's hardly enough room for us in our flat as it is.' She thought of Robbie's burst football collection that filled their room and was soon to be joined by his new collections of giant shells, pebbles and feathers.

'True,' said Opal. 'There's not enough room to swing a camel in your flat.'

'It's not a camel you swing,' said Martha, 'it's a cat. And we haven't even got room for one of those.

136

Mum's always telling us we can't have a pet because the flat isn't big enough, so how can there be space for a whole other person? I bet Sam would want to bring a load of stuff with him, too.'

'Like what sort of stuff?' said Robbie.

'I don't know. Piles of extra swimming trunks or nose pegs or whatever swimming instructors have. More of his stinky, pooey trainers!'

Robbie and Opal giggled. Martha laughed at herself a bit, too. She couldn't think what Sam might bring with him, but it wasn't really his stuff that bothered her. It was the idea of Sam having his own front-door key, Sam moving in and living with them for good. It would be such a massive change. A change she wasn't at all sure she would like.

'Are you going to bowl that ball, Martha?' called Sam from his fielding position, way back up the beach.

'Yes, I am!' she yelled. She drew back her arm and threw the ball as hard as she could at Opal's bat. It felt good throwing the ball, almost as if she was chucking her bottled-up thoughts away with it. It hit the bat with a resounding *clack*!

'Cow's eye!' shouted Opal as the ball soared into the sky.

Sam hared off into the distance with Garnet bombing after him, while Opal skipped and hopped her way around the jumpers. 'A rounder!' she whooped, as she reached the fourth one. 'I made my

137

first whole rounder! A rounder, a rounder!'

They were just taking their positions again for the next ball when Sam said, 'Hold up, what's wrong with the little guy?'

Garnet was still far off, up the beach. 'Here, boy, here,' Sam called. Normally when you called him, Garnet came hurtling back like a jet-propelled cushion, but not today.

They all tried calling him, but Garnet didn't move.

'Oh, crumbles!' said Opal, letting the rounders bat fall to her side. 'That's ripped it!'

'What?' said Martha.

'I think it's started.'

'What do you mean? What's started?' Opal didn't answer, but the pinched expression on her face gave Martha a horrible sinking feeling. Something was wrong. Something to do with Garnet.

Opal dropped the bat on the sand and began to run. Martha had never seen her look so horror-stricken. She ran after her. Was the secret Opal had wanted to keep from her about to be uncovered?

Garnet was lying in a very peculiar way. All four of his legs were stretched out sideways and he had gone very flat, as flat as a fluffy bathmat.

Robbie reached him first. 'What's up, Garnie?' he said. 'You missing Bonnie-Belle-Flower-Lady again? Is that it?'

Garnet thumped his stubby tail twice, but he didn't lift his head off the sand.

'He's not himself, is he?' Sam sounded concerned.

Garnet's lynx ears, normally so sharp and upright, drooped on his head.

Gingerly, Martha touched his little pink nose. 'It's dry,' she said.

'That's not a good sign in a dog,' said Sam, who, like everyone else, still thought Garnet was Opal's pet dog. 'Maybe he's had too much sun. Why don't you find him some shade?'

Mum joined them, her fingers still marking her place in her book. 'He could be dehydrated. I've got a bottle of water. Let's look for a shell to put it in, so he can have a drink.'

'Thank you, Marie Stephens,' said Opal. Martha thought her voice sounded a bit shaky. 'But I'll take him straight back to the campsite, if you don't mind.' She picked Garnet up. He was floppy in her arms, and a breeze ruffled his fur this way and that. He looked as weak and helpless as a tiny baby.

'We'll all go up,' said Mum, pulling her cardigan round herself. 'It's getting chilly. I think the weather's on the turn.'

'Yes.' Opal glanced out over the horizon. 'It's already raining cats and frogs in Ireland. Storm's coming our way, too.'

Mum smiled in amusement but Opal looked grave. She led the way up the hill back to the campsite, taking such long strides that Martha and Robbie struggled to keep up.

'Do you think Garnie's eyes look different?' Robbie puffed as he trotted along. 'Sort of cloudy? Do you think he's sick? He's not sick, is he, Martha? Do mingles get sick, do you think?'

Her little brother looked so nervous, Martha wanted to reassure him, but she couldn't. She felt panicky herself.

'I don't know,' she panted back at him. 'But something's really, really wrong. I'm sure of it.'

'Let us know if you want to take him to a vet, Opal, won't you?' said Mum when they reached the campsite.

'Righty-ho, Marie Stephens.' Opal spoke over her shoulder as she hurried back to her parachute tent. The yellow material rippled in the wind.

'Yes,' said Sam. 'I'd be happy to drive you.'

'Thanks, Sam the Man,' said Opal, still not stopping. She slid away under the parachute.

'We'll be in here if you need us,' called Mum, unzipping their tent. 'Sam and I've got something to talk about actually, so maybe we should all hunker down this afternoon. Might not be a bad idea, considering.' She nodded at the clouds whipping towards them across the ocean.

Martha followed Opal under the edge of the parachute silk.

Opal was standing in the middle of the Domestipod, stroking Garnet's head. Her violet eyes were shadowy with sadness.

'This is it, Martha,' she said softly.

'The secret?' Martha whispered back.

Opal nodded.

'What secret?' said Robbie, coming into the Domestipod and looking from one girl's face to the other. 'Why are there so many secrets, suddenly? I didn't know Opal had a secret.'

'I won't have,' Opal said. 'Not in a minute. And there won't be any more secrets after this one. It's too late for secrets now.'

A horrible heavy feeling dropped all the way from Martha's throat to her stomach. She dreaded hearing what the secret was. It was obviously going to be something terrible. She was so afraid she was about to hear bad news about Garnet. But, however bad the news was, she was determined to help in whatever way she could. Not hearing it wasn't an option.

'Tell us, Opal,' she said. 'Please. Just tell us what it is!'

When Opal finished her story, neither Martha nor Robbie could speak. They sat in silence for a long time, staring miserably at the silver cube in the corner. It was still bright outside, but in the Domestipod, the world seemed dark and bleak.

At last Robbie said, 'So that's what a Minmangulator looks like.'

'Yup,' said Opal.

There was another long silence. Martha broke it eventually, saying, 'And you're just supposed to . . . to post him? Into that hole?'

'Yup,' said Opal again. They all gazed at the flap at the top of the cube. Martha imagined the flap flicking inwards as it opened and then snapping shut again, so that not a chink of light could disturb the

darkness that lay inside.

'I can't believe it,' she said. 'I think it's cruel.'

'It's awful,' Robbie croaked. Martha thought he might be about to cry. She felt like crying herself.

Even Opal, who never cried, looked extra pale. 'Cruel?' she repeated. 'I never used to think it was cruel. I put the rest of my mingles in there without a second thought. I didn't miss them, either, not for a milli-moment. Out of sight was out of brain. I feel different now, though.'

'You can't do it, Opal!' Robbie burst out. 'You can't do it. Not to Garnet!' He crawled over to where Opal was now sitting cross-legged, with Garnet curled up and snoozing in her lap. He stroked the mingle's head over and over, sneezing as he did so. 'You can't put Garnet back in the Minmangulator. I won't – *achoo* – let you!'

'I don't *want* to do it, Cucumber Hero,' said Opal sadly, giving Robbie the nickname she had made up for him long ago. 'But I have to. It's Carnelian Law.'

'But why?' asked Martha. 'Why does everybody have to re-minmangulate their mingles? Why can't they keep them forever?'

Opal had explained that when mingles were one year old, their owners were supposed to put them back in the Minmangulator; they were supposed to mix up fresh new ones. Martha understood now why Uncle Bixbite's mingle was different from before. It was because the old one had gone past its use-by date; it had been dropped into the Minmangulator, never to be seen again. Like a piece of old cheese, Martha thought, being tossed, unwanted, into the bin.

'Why don't Carnelians want to keep their mingles forever? That's what we'd do, wouldn't we, Robbie, if we had a pet?'

Robbie sucked in his lips and nodded. He was too choked up to speak.

'That's because you're human beings, with spongy hearts and overactive emotions,' Opal answered. 'It's different where I come from. You see, after a year, mingles start dwindling. Things begin to go wrong with them. We have to re-minmangulate them before that can happen. On Carnelia, logic is king.'

'King-shming!' said Robbie fiercely. 'Logic isn't king. That's stupid and rubbish! Anyway,' he protested, 'so what if things *do* go wrong with the mingles? Don't you have vets, or repair shops? Places you can get them fixed?'

'It wouldn't be logical to do that,' Opal replied. 'Things that have been fixed often break again. It's much more efficient to trade in your mingle and make a spanking grand new one. We're not allowed to keep them longer than a year. It's against Carnelian Law.'

'Well, I hate Carnelian Law,' Robbie shouted. 'Carnelian Law should be outlawed!'

'Robbie's right,' said Martha. 'I'm sorry, Opal, I

know it's your planet and everything, but that's a horrible law. It's cruel!'

Opal didn't answer, but Martha saw from the expression on her face that she agreed.

Martha looked again at the Minmangulator. 'So . . . the mingles go in there,' she said, touching the flap with the very tip of her finger. She wanted to be sure she had understood. 'And that's . . .' she dropped her voice to a whisper, afraid Garnet might hear her even in his sleep, '. . . that's the *end* of them?'

Opal sighed. 'Not the very absolute, final end. Once they're inside the Minmangulator, they get unmingled. Then their different qualities and properties can be mixed up again and they come out as something completely different.'

'Like recycling,' said Martha, thinking of the plastic box they filled each week at home with empty cans and jars. It was her job to take it down to the big green recycling bin outside the flats. She had to separate out the glass things from the metal things and then post them into the right holes in the recycling bin. She quite enjoyed doing that, but she couldn't imagine putting a living creature in one of the holes. It would be impossible.

'What's changed, though?' Martha asked. 'How come you could re-minmangulate your other mingles, and now you don't want to do it?'

'I've been wondering about that,' said Opal. 'I think it's something to do with the number of

146

hours I've spent on Earth.' She smiled sadly. 'You sentimental humans are a bad influenza on me!'

Robbie sneezed. 'Garnet's never going in there!' he said. 'I won't let you do it, Opal. Not ever! If you put Garnie in there, I'll . . . I'll do anything . . . I'll jam the machine!'

'He has to go in, I'm afraid, Cucumber Hero,' Opal said. 'He does. I've twisted the rules of Carnelian Law long enough. I did it so that I could spend as much time with him as possible. I wanted to stroke his little head and see him spin it round three hundred and sixty degrees. I wanted to watch him run and jump and fly, and have fun with his new friend.'

Martha thought of Garnet showing his wings to Bonnie-Belle-Flower-Lady. She remembered the two animals playing together at the Fete. It seemed a very long time ago.

'I wanted to feel the warmth of his stripy, spotty tummy when he turned over for a tickle,' Opal went on. 'It's completely illogical, and you'll think I'm a silly witnit, but I even wanted to keep on smelling his musky, furry smell. I want to smell it for as long as I can.' She buried her nose in Garnet's soft fur.

Martha didn't think Opal was a nitwit at all. She wanted to do all those things, too. She never wanted to stop doing them. She never wanted to let him go. The thought of it reminded her that it wasn't only Garnet she would have to let go. Soon she would have to let go of Opal, as well.

'I love Garnet,' she whispered. 'We all do.'

'Trouble is,' Opal went on, 'he's already weaker than he used to be. I can't let him get too feeble, or he might fade away altogether.' She glanced up at the light shade, biting her bottom lip. 'And if my mingle fades away, then . . .'

'. . . then so will you,' finished Martha. She felt cold as the realisation dawned on her. If Garnet became very ill and died while he was on Earth, so would Opal.

'That's right,' said Opal. 'I knew you'd realise that, Martha. That's why I didn't want to tell you about all this. I'm sorry I kept you in the shade, but I knew you'd ask me to put Garnet in the Minmangulator. I knew you'd want to do the right thing.'

Martha was flabbergasted. '*That* was why you kept it a secret?' she spluttered.

Opal nodded sadly.

Tears pricked at Martha's eyes, she was so shocked by what Opal had just said. It was true that she had tried to get Opal to stick to Uncle Bixbite's rules, but that was only to help her get her CIA. She would never have encouraged her to do away with Garnet like this, not in a million zillion years.

'I wouldn't have done that, Opal! I wouldn't have made you put him in. I wouldn't!'

'Wouldn't you?'

'No! How could you think that about me?' It was as if Opal had forgotten she had feelings.

Opal looked sheepish. 'I'm sorry. Maybe I don't understand human hearts. It's just, you've always been so good at making sure I do everything properly to get my CIA. I thought you'd be bound to take Uncle Bixbite's side.'

Martha wondered if it was true, but only for a moment. She knew she could never have tried to persuade Opal to do such a thing.

'You should have trusted me, Opal. You should have told me before. I wish you had. I might have been able to help.'

'I'm sorry, Martha,' Opal moaned. 'I'm sorry I didn't. I don't know how I could have been such a blunder-nut!' Garnet wheezed in her lap. 'But it makes no difference now. I don't have a choice any more. Now is the time.'

'No!' Robbie cried. 'It's OK. He's not that bad. Not yet. He's a bit poorly, that's all, having an off day. He might just be hungry. Look, I've brought him a treat.' He reached around behind him and pulled a packet of bacon from the waistband of his shorts.

'Where did that come from?' Martha said.

'Sam's cool box. He won't mind, he likes Garnie.'

Robbie pulled out a rasher of bacon and waved it in front of Garnet's nose. 'Here, boy,' he said. 'Look, it's your favourite. Yummy, yummy bacon. Mmm!'

Garnet raised his head and touched the slimy rasher with his nose. He licked it twice, but the licks were very half-hearted and Martha could see he was only doing it to please Robbie.

'It really is too late,' said Opal. 'I'm afraid Garnie is travelling downhill fast. We can't put it off any longer.' She began to stand up.

'Wait!' said Martha. 'Not yet, please. There must be something we can do.' It was all happening so quickly. Their wonderful summer holiday was suddenly coming to a horrible, horrible end. She had to come up with a way to stop this awful thing from happening.

'Please, just let me think.' She pressed her face into her hands and tried to concentrate. They couldn't take Garnet to a vet, that was for certain. No Earth vet would know how to treat a mingle, in any case, and once they looked at Garnet closely they would find out he was a mixed-up animal, and then Opal's alien identity would be discovered and there'd be more trouble than Martha could even imagine.

She looked up. 'What about medicine? I'll get the First Aid pack; there's bound to be something in there.'

Opal shook her head. 'There's no cure,' she said. 'There's nothing that can help Garnie now.'

'At least let us try, Opal!' Martha cried. 'You never know, we might be able to think of something you haven't.'

Martha put her face back in her hands and tried to gather her thoughts, but they were all over the place. Through her fingers she saw Robbie trying again to tempt Garnet with the bacon. He sounded as if he was talking to a baby. 'Come on,' he was saying. 'Try some. Just have an ickle-lickle bit. It's really good for you, you know. Bacon's a superfood, most probably.'

'Robbie!' Martha said suddenly, grabbing his shoulder. 'What about that stuff Sam showed us?'

'What stuff?'

'You know, that weird green stuff he found down at the beach. He said that was a superfood. Remember? He said it could cure loads of illnesses.'

'Oh, that,' said Robbie. 'It was called . . . Sam's fire, I think.'

'Not Sam's fire, no, not that. Nearly, but . . .' Martha racked her brains, wishing for once that she had paid more attention to the things Sam had told them when they were exploring the rocks.

'Rock samphire!' she pounced on the words. 'That's it, rock samphire!' She turned to Opal. 'Maybe we could give Garnet some of that. It might make him better.'

'There's no cure, though, Martha,' Opal said again.

'You don't know that. Not for sure. Maybe on Carnelia there isn't anything that would help, but there might be something on Earth. We won't know unless we try.' Now that she had had the idea, she was determined to try it out. She just needed to convince Opal to give them time to do it.

'Have a go if you like,' said Opal. 'I think we can risk another hour or so. What is this rock samphire, anyway?'

'It grows wild round here,' Martha explained. 'It's got leaves like fat little fingers and yellowy flowers that look like old broccoli. It stinks of petrol, but Sam says it can kill poisons and purify blood.'

'He only found a tiny bit of it on the rocks though,' said Robbie. 'I don't know if there is any more.'

'Leaves like fingers, you say? And yellowy flowers?' Opal looked through the window of the Domestipod.

Robbie and Martha looked that way too. All they could see was the wall of bright dandelion yellow made by Mrs Underedge's parachute silk, but Opal seemed to be looking much further than that; she looked as if she was gazing far into the distance, scanning the whole countryside.

'Banjo!' she declared after a moment. 'I can see it! I can see a whole load of it.'

'Where?' said Martha and Robbie together.

'There's a big patch clinging to the rock, near the bottom. It's in the next cove along, the one shaped like half a cheese and onion crisp.'

'That's Nohaven,' said Martha, her heart sinking as she recognised the description. 'But there's no way down from up here. We'd have to go right round the headland. Opal, is the tide in or out at the moment? Can you see?'

'It's out,' said Opal, 'but we don't need to go round. I'll go and get it. I can shin down the cliff and pick that stuff in an instant. You'll hardly know I've gone.'

She was halfway to the door when Martha pulled her back. 'No! We promised Mum we wouldn't climb on the cliffs. It's too dangerous. And you shouldn't go at all, Opal. You need to be with Garnet, and he's too sick to go anywhere. We can't risk him getting any worse. I'll go. I'll have to go the long way round, but I'm a fast runner. I promise I'll be as quick as I can.'

Before the others could protest, Martha ran out of the Domestipod.

'I'll rest an eye on you, Martha,' she heard Opal call as she slipped under the parachute silk.

She began pelting across the field, but then remembered she had nothing in which to carry the rock samphire. If it did make Garnet better, he would need a good supply and the pockets of her shorts wouldn't be big enough. She nipped into Sam's tent and grabbed her red backpack which lay just by the entrance.

'Where are you off to in such a hurry?' Martha had forgotten that Mum and Sam were in there. They were kneeling together on the groundsheet, filling a cardboard box with tins and packets, ready for when they left the next morning.

'I'm just going to . . . to pick some wild food,' said Martha. She couldn't tell them where she was really going. She was pretty sure Mum would stop her if she knew what she was planning. She realised she felt quite shaky.

'Good for you, Martha,' Sam was saying. 'You get foraging and bring back supper!' He began searching through one of the boxes. 'Tea bags in here anywhere, Marie?'

'Well,' said Mum, still looking at Martha, 'you know it's going to rain soon.' She sounded doubtful. Martha was terrified she was going to stop her from going. She *had* to go. Garnet was depending on her now. They all were.

'I thought I'd look for that samphire stuff,' she said, trying to sound casual, and hoping her legs didn't look as trembly as they felt. 'Like you showed us, Sam.'

Mum nodded thoughtfully and oh, so slowly! Martha could tell she wasn't sure about letting her go, but she seemed pleased that Martha was doing something Sam had suggested for once.

'All right,' she said at last. Martha was already halfway out of the tent when Mum called her back again. 'But, Martha—'

'Yes?' she said, desperate to run.

'Don't go too far. And don't go eating anything before you've shown it to Sam or me, OK?'

'OK,' Martha called, slinging her bag over her shoulder and running towards the footpath that led down to the beach. She could see from the way the sand was shining that the tide was already completely out. If she was going to make it back to Garnet and the others before it came in again, she would have to move fast. Very fast.

14

Martha could have made it down to the beach much more quickly if it hadn't been for all the holidaymakers coming back up. Three times she had to stop and stand to the side while little family groups plodded up the path, lugging windbreaks and cool boxes and pulling straggling toddlers behind them. She wanted to tell them to hurry, that she was on an extremely important mission, a matter of life and death. But she couldn't say that so she had to wait, hopping about in the grass, until the moment when she could dart forward again.

Once down, she hurtled over the sand. The wind was in her face and made the empty backpack flap up and down on her shoulder so that she felt like a one-winged bird urgently trying to take off. If only

she *could* fly!

She crossed Stormhaven bay in record time, slowing only a little when she reached the headland. The sea was a long way off, but it wouldn't be long before the tide turned. She ran on, passing a large boulder that stood about halfway across the sand. She hadn't noticed the boulder before – it must only be visible at low tide. She skirted round it, making her legs go faster than they wanted to go. She fell over once, but picked herself up quickly and stumbled on. If only she could get the samphire, if only Garnet would eat it, that might be the answer. She wanted to prove to Opal that she didn't care about doing the right thing, whatever that was. She just wanted the best for Garnet. She just wanted to save him.

She glanced up at the steep rock face. She knew Robbie and Opal were at the campsite, urging her onwards. 'I'm almost there. Hold on, Garnie!' she shouted.

At last she rounded the headland and arrived in Nohaven bay. It really was a tiny cove. There was hardly space on the beach to spread a picnic rug. Apart from a single seagull that waddled along on the sand, it was completely deserted.

Almost immediately, Martha saw the clump of samphire Opal had spotted. It was growing in a shallow hollow, on a stretch of gently sloping rock. She leaped onto the rock, dodging pools of seawater, working her way upwards until she reached the patch of greeny-yellow vegetation.

'Shoo!' she shouted at the seagull, which had flown ahead of her and was pecking at the precious samphire. She waved her arms at it. 'Sorry, but I need it more than you do. You find something else.'

The seagull flapped away and Martha tugged the plants from the rock. She crammed them whole, flowers and all, into her backpack until it was stuffed like a fat pillow. It felt good to have it safely in her bag, but there was no time to relax. This was her chance to save Garnet. Her one chance.

She hooked the full bag over her shoulder and scrambled back down the rocky slope. She slipped once and scraped her leg hard on rock, or shells. She didn't stop to find out which, but got to her feet immediately. She didn't know how they were going to feed the samphire to Garnet, whether he could eat it raw or whether they would have to cook it first. The main thing was to get it to him as quickly as possible.

But when Martha reached the headland again, she was shocked to see that the tide had already turned. The water was surging towards her in an alarming way. She ran on as the first few delicate waves washed casually over her toes. The water made her slither around in her flip-flops, so she took them off and put them on her hands. She kept telling herself that she would be fine, that the water wasn't really getting deeper already, it wasn't really up to her calves, it definitely wasn't up to her knees. That was just her imagination. It had to be.

It was getting harder and harder to run. She jumped and splashed her way through the water. Then, as it reached her thighs, she had to wade. She battled on, using the flip-flops on her hands as paddles, hardly daring to think what would happen if she didn't make it back to Stormhaven beach before full tide.

Ahead of her, she saw waves hitting the boulder in the sand, rushing round it until it was surrounded by water. Martha wasn't even level with the boulder yet, and the water was already up to her waist. She bobbed up and down, her toes reaching for the sand at every step, but her progress was too slow like that. She had to start swimming. That would be fine, she told herself. It wouldn't matter if the samphire got wet; it grew by the sea, it got wet all the time. She let her flip-flops go and tried not to notice them being carried out to sea. She tried to concentrate on Garnet and the samphire instead.

Martha had swum out of her depth loads of times. Once you could swim it made no difference how deep you went, but this was different. The water was pulling and dragging at her body. The more she swam forwards, the more it tugged her sideways, hauling her off course.

At last she reached the boulder. Its top was rough and gnarled and Martha found a hole to hook her fingers into and hung on. She didn't have time to stop but swimming was such hard work, she needed to catch her breath. She would only rest for a few seconds.

Glancing behind her, she saw that the water seemed choppy and troubled; it was travelling and rippling all over the place, not just in the direction of the coast. She remembered what Sam had said about rip tides that developed with the wind and could sweep swimmers out to sea.

For the first time, Martha felt afraid, not just for Garnet and Opal but for herself. Why hadn't she told Sam and Mum where she was going? It had been stupid not to. She could have kicked herself. She needed to swim on, but the undertow of the water was too much. She knew that if she let go of the rock she would be swept immediately out to sea, just as her flip-flops had been.

With a great effort she hauled herself upwards onto the top of the boulder. She stood on it, shivering, her toes clutching barnacles as she tried not to slip. Carefully she took the backpack off and tried to squeeze some of the water out of it. At least she still had the samphire. There was still a chance of getting it to Garnet. If she didn't drown first.

Now her breathing was almost back to normal. Stormhaven beach wasn't far away, but she couldn't see it so it must already be underwater. The sea rushed around her, slapping at her boulder, spitting spray. Martha knew she couldn't go on with the sea like that – she didn't dare. She was trapped.

'Stop it!' Martha yelled at the swirling water. She was furious with the sea for thwarting her, and furious with herself for being too slow.

'Stupid!' she shouted. 'Let me go! You let me go!'

She didn't know why she was shouting at the sea; it couldn't hear her. No one could. There was no one even in sight. And, anyway, her cries were swallowed by the wind. Calling for help would be useless.

She wondered how long she could stay here. How long would it be before the boulder was completely covered by water? Did she have hours, or only minutes? She wondered the same thing about Garnet. She didn't know how long he had left, either. Opal and Robbie might already have given up on her. They might be putting Garnet in the Minmangulator at this very moment. She would never see him again. Maybe she would never see Opal again either, or Robbie, or even Mum.

Around her, rain poured down like tears. 'I'm so sorry, Opal,' Martha murmured. Her attempt to save Garnet had been a disaster. 'I'm so sorry.'

At that moment, a voice rang out from above.

'Nothing to apologise for, Martha. Hold on now. I'm on my zooming way!'

Blinking rain from her eyes, Martha looked up to see Opal climbing rapidly down the cliff face towards her. Looking higher, she saw Robbie and

Garnet, both lying flat on the grass at the top of the cliff, their anxious faces peering over the edge. Garnet was still alive.

Martha felt a surge of relief and hope fill her chest. She should have realised Opal would have been watching her. Opal had seen the trouble she was in. She and Robbie must have run across the fields to find her. To rescue her. She should have remembered she wasn't doing all this alone. She was part of a team. The best team in the world.

Suddenly Opal let go of the rock and dropped. Martha gasped, sure she was about to plunge into the sea, but Opal landed neatly on a narrow ledge a couple of metres above the water. She faced Martha, her back pressing against the rock, her hair whipping around her head as she was buffeted by the growing wind.

'Soon have you out of there, Martha. Catch hold!'

She opened her eyes very wide and a bright ray of violet light shot out of them. The light ray rippled across the sea like a streamer. The end of it landed in the water in front of Martha.

'Come on, Martha,' Opal was clutching the other end of the ray in her hands now, winding it round her arm. Now Martha understood what was happening. Opal was throwing her a lifeline. It was up to her to catch it, then Opal would pull her back to the headland. She knelt on the boulder and leant out as far as she dared, snatching at the water as the purple line floated near her. But she couldn't quite reach. Each time she thought she had it, a new wave came and whipped the line away from her fingers.

Water was sloshing right over the boulder now. Even on her hands and knees, Martha was starting to lose her grip. And however hard she tried, however often she lunged for it, she still couldn't reach the lifeline.

She tried to shout, 'I can't do it, Opal!' But when she opened her mouth, a big wave rushed at her, knocking her sideways, and she inhaled salty water, which made her cough and splutter.

She thought she might be about to drown. She began to shake. She was so very cold and so very, very afraid.

'Don't be afraid!' Opal shouted. 'I'll save you, Martha, no matter what! If my eye power won't do the job, I'll do it myself!' She bent her knees and prepared to launch herself off the ledge.

'No!' Martha shrieked. 'You mustn't, Opal! You can't swim!'

Swimming in the sand was one thing, but Opal had never even tried swimming in the sea.

'Please, don't jump,' Martha begged. 'You mustn't risk your life, Opal. Please! Stay where you are!'

'No, Martha, I will not! Not on your Neddy!'

Opal bent lower, ready to spring.

Martha screamed. Something was falling from above. For a dreadful split second she thought it was

Robbie; she thought he had fallen off the top of the cliff and was plummeting to the sea. Then she heard a terrified yell from above and Martha, recognising her brother's cry, saw that he wasn't the one who was falling after all. He was still up there, looking down, wailing, 'No! No! No!'

Whatever was tumbling out of the sky was much smaller and lighter than a boy, and it wasn't falling so much as floating, floating on outspread blue-grey wings.

✷ ✶ ✶

As he neared the sea, Garnet folded his wings and pointed his nose downwards, gathering speed, so that when he hit the water it was with such force that he dived right down, plunging to the sand at the bottom.

'Garnie!' Martha breathed as he came to the surface, a shining violet rope gripped in his jaws. He paddled towards her, using his wings as oars, somehow managing to keep a steady course, and put his snout in her hand. Her fingers closed over his wet muzzle and Martha grasped the lifeline Opal's eyes had sent her. She didn't know how Garnet had found the strength to bring it to her. She was supposed to be saving his life, but now he was saving hers.

She picked him up and put him round her neck, then she took hold of the line with both hands and flung herself into the water. She was shivering uncontrollably now, but she swam as best she could while Opal hauled on the line, pulling her back to the rock. At last she reached it, and with Opal's help climbed painfully up to join her on the ledge.

'I'm OK!' she gasped. 'I'm OK, Opal.' It felt so good to be out of the water; it was such a relief, she found she was almost laughing. She hugged Opal.

Opal hugged her back, but Martha soon realised that Opal wasn't sharing in her sudden joy. She was staring at Martha's neck.

Reaching up, Martha touched wet, cold fur. She took Garnet from her neck and passed him to Opal. He was heavy, like a sponge soaked in water, and he looked terrible. His wings lay open, one of them bent back awkwardly. His body was limp and his amber eyes were closed.

It was only then that Martha remembered the samphire. They had to give him some now before it was too late. She put a hand to her shoulder where the backpack should be.

It was gone.

Martha searched the ledge at her feet, but it wasn't there either. She looked round wildly and caught sight of a red blob, whirling through the water, being carried out to sea. The backpack must have fallen off her shoulder in the swim. She'd never even noticed.

'I've lost the samphire!'

Opal looked at her. 'I know.'

Martha stared. It had all been for nothing. She had

found all that lovely samphire, and then she had gone and let it go. Now there was nothing they could do.

'Garnie! Garnie!'

Martha looked up at Robbie calling out from above.

He was standing on the clifftop, rubbing at his eyes. Martha could see he was crying. She knew why, too. He thought Garnet was dead. Garnet was lying so still, she thought he might be right. And if Garnet was dead, if she had no mingle, then it wouldn't be long before Opal died too.

15

Martha clutched her head with her hands.
'I'm so, so sorry, Opal!' The whole rescue
attempt had been for nothing. It was all hopeless.
They had lost Garnet, and now they were going to
lose Opal, too.

'Steady up, Martha. I'm not completely ready to
toss in the flannel, you know.'

'What?'

Martha glanced quickly at Opal. She was still
standing; she hadn't slumped to the side or fallen
over or anything, so it couldn't be true. Garnet must
be alive.

Opal put her hands on Garnet's waterlogged
body. 'Yes,' she said. 'He is. But only just. His heart
has nine hundred and thirty-one beats left. I'll have

to put him in the Minmangulator now, Martha. Otherwise . . .'

Her voice trailed away. They both knew what would happen otherwise.

It was too unfair on Garnet. He'd done so much for Opal, and for Martha too. If it wasn't for him she would still be stuck on that boulder, but Martha knew there was nothing more they could do for him. They had to put him in the Minmangulator to save Opal's life. Opal was the one they had to concentrate on now.

'We'd better get him back to the Domestipod quickly,' Martha said, trying to be brave. 'But how?'

She looked down at the waves frothing at the bottom of the cliff like a white frill on the hem of a party dress. She couldn't see any way of getting back round to the safety of Stormhaven cove. She wondered how long it would take for Garnet's heart to beat nine hundred and thirty-one times. Was it longer than it would take for the tide to go out far enough for them to make their way back along the beach? If they waited for that, would they still have time to put Garnet in the Minmangulator and save Opal's life?

'No,' said Opal, reading her thoughts. 'Not nearly enough time. We'll have to go that way.' She pointed upwards and commanded, 'Stand forward, Cucumber Hero. We need your help.'

Martha saw Robbie come to the edge of the cliff again. She could tell he was biting his nails.

'Important task for you,' Opal called. 'Catch hold of this rope.'

Martha was just about to say, 'What rope?' when a long and luminous purple string darted out of Opal's eyes and catapulted up the cliff, just like the one that had shot out into the sea. Robbie dived on it, trapping it under his body. He scrambled to his feet and held up the end of the shining rope for Opal to see. 'Got it!' he yelled.

'Good. Now take the rope, run to the Domestipod and tie it to the door knocker.'

Robbie hesitated. 'I . . . I'm not that good at knots,' he said.

'Just do it,' Martha shouted. 'You've got to!'

'You can do it, Cucumber Hero,' Opal said. 'I know you can. Now run like the breeze!'

Robbie sped away. Martha wondered what people would think if they saw her brother running across the fields with a rope that shone like the moon. She hardly cared about that now: as long as the rope helped them get Garnet to the Minmangulator in time, that was all that mattered. No sooner did she think about it, though, than the rope lost its light and dulled to a plain matt purple.

'Now it's the same as any Earth climbing rope,' said Opal, tugging on the rope to check it was secure. 'He's done it.' She stood behind Martha and looped the rope around their waists, tying them firmly together.

Martha looked up at the sheer cliff face and swallowed.

'Maybe you could go on your own,' she said, feeling suddenly sick. 'I could stay here and wait for the tide to go out a bit. Then I could join you.'

'No,' said Opal. 'You can't stay here, Martha. This ledge will soon be covered in seawater.'

Martha looked at the cliff and saw a line stretching all the way across the rock just above their heads. The rock above the line was light grey; patches of lichen grew there and tiny bits of grass stuck out of the cracks. Below the line, though, the rock was very dark. Nothing grew on it at all, and the only things clinging to it, apart from the two of them, were blue-black mussels that wouldn't be the least bit concerned by the arrival of the sea. Opal was right. Waiting on the ledge wasn't an option.

'I'll take care of you.' Opal put Garnet into Martha's arms. 'You hold Garnie,' she said, 'and I'll do the rest.' She pulled the rope tight.

Martha hated the cliff, but she knew they had to get to the top of it. She had to trust Opal. And she did trust her. She trusted that the rope was strong and that it was tied firmly to the Domestipod's door knocker. She trusted that her friend would not let her go. She didn't know if she would have felt the same a few days before. She had always looked out for Opal. She had got used to doing that. It had never really been the other way around.

But there was something about Opal that was different today. She seemed stronger somehow, in control. It dawned on Martha that she would trust Opal with anything. She would trust her with her life. She *was* trusting her with her life.

'I trust you too, Martha,' Opal said. 'Totally and absolutely. I'll never not trust you again. Now, lean on me.'

Martha felt herself drawn backwards, further and further, until the soles of her feet rested flat against the cliff. She kept her eyes closed and imagined how she and Opal must look, lying in the air at a right angle to the rock, in the shape of a perfect capital L.

'What now?' she cried nervously.

'Now we walk,' said Opal. Her right leg pushed against Martha's right leg. For a moment, Martha resisted, unable to lift her foot. 'Come on,' Opal whispered into her ear, 'you can do it. It's not far to the top – it's only a hop, squat and a jump.'

Martha screwed up her face to make herself braver and, trying not to think of falling, took her foot off the wall of rock.

Immediately her leg was pushed upwards through the air by Opal's leg and when she put her foot down again, it was a little higher up the rock. Then Opal pressed her left leg against Martha's left leg and she moved that one too.

They kept on like that, left, right, left, right, moving as stiffly and slowly as robots. But they weren't robots. They were a human girl and an alien girl with a million feelings coursing through their bodies, a million thoughts buzzing in their heads. Martha could feel Opal's arms moving round her own as she pulled on the rope, hand over hand over hand, until finally they reached the top of the cliff.

As soon as the hard rock turned to soft grass beneath her feet, Martha felt herself being tipped upright again. She opened her eyes to see Robbie heaving wildly on the rope. He didn't seem to notice that she and Opal had already reached the top of the cliff, and he kept hauling the rope so that Martha ran right into him, knocking him to the ground and stumbling on top of him. Opal, still tied together with Martha, fell too, and the three of them lay sprawled in an uncomfortable heap.

Garnet's head rolled loosely in Martha's hands. He opened his eyes and wheezed *chi-cha*.

'Garnet's alive!' Robbie said breathlessly, sitting up and picking grass from his tongue. 'That's so brilliant! Where's the samphire, Martha? Have you given him any of it yet?'

'I lost it.' Martha bit her lip. 'I'm so sorry, Robbie.' Robbie adored Garnet as much as she did. Maybe even more.

But Robbie didn't seem to understand. 'He will be OK though, won't he? Is he going to—'

'He's going in the Minmangulator,' said Opal before he could finish.

'But—' Robbie's face crumpled.

'We have to, Robbie,' Martha said. 'If we don't he'll die anyway, and Opal will be left without a mingle. And you know what that means!' She was telling herself as much as him. This was the only way now. But her words sounded awful, hard and cold to her own ears.

Robbie didn't speak. He just threw the end of the rope away from him, over the edge of the cliff.

'Yes,' said Opal, calmly taking Garnet from Martha. 'I'm afraid the time for shelly-shollying is over. Only six hundred and eight heartbeats left.' She got to her feet and said solemnly, 'Come, Earth dwellers. It's time.' Cuddling Garnet to her, she started to run across the field.

Whatever she and Robbie felt now, however heavy their feet, Martha knew there was nothing to do but follow Opal.

16

Opal, Martha and Robbie ran as fast as they could across the field and onto the campsite. It was raining hard. No one else was about.

Martha half expected to see Mum and Sam out looking for them, but they were still in their tent, sitting on Sam's folding camp stools. She couldn't see their faces as she ran past, just their knees, which were almost touching, and the mugs which they held clasped on their laps. The kettle was still steaming on the little outdoor stove. So much had happened, Martha felt as though she had been away from the campsite for hours. But it could only have been a matter of minutes.

They slithered under the parachute silk, and a moment later they were standing inside the

Domestipod, staring at the Minmangulator.

Opal, cradling Garnet in one arm, lifted two purple cloaks from her clothes rail. It was only when she draped the first one around her freezing shoulders that Martha realised how much she was trembling. Trembling not just with cold, but with the horrible knowledge of what they had to do next. Opal put a cloak on Robbie, too, and Martha saw that his eyes were round with terror.

Only Opal looked strong and sure of herself.

Garnet lay like a baby in her arms, gazing at her with his amber eyes. She smiled down at him. 'It's time,' she said. She walked over to Robbie and held Garnet out to him. Martha saw tears well up in Robbie's eyes as he reached out and stroked Garnet's tummy. He knew he was doing it for the last time.

'G-goodbye, Garnie,' he managed to say. Martha felt her own eyes smarting as Garnet answered with a faint *chi-wee*.

She thought her heart might break when she heard that little noise. She thought of how much fun they had all had with Garnet. He would never play with them or anyone ever again.

Robbie sneezed. 'I wouldn't mind sneezing – *achoo* – forever if it meant you could stay.' He stuck his nose in Garnet's damp fur and sneezed some more.

Then it was Martha's turn. Opal held Garnet out to her and she touched the rough fur on the ridge of his nose. 'I'll never forget you,' she whispered through her tears. They were falling freely now, but she didn't care about that. 'I'll never forget you, not for as long as I live.'

Martha still didn't really understand how the Minmangulator worked, or where the different parts of Garnet were going to end up, but she knew they were going to lose him. She thought of the very first time she had seen him, when she had first met Opal in the ground-floor flats on the Half Moon Estate. She hadn't believed Opal was an alien then, or that Garnet was a mingle. She had spent ages poring over her animal encyclopaedia looking for an animal that resembled him, but of course she had never found one. There was only one Garnet. And that made what they were about to do to him all the worse.

'Darn it, Garnet,' said Opal softly as she bent over him. Her voice was sad but it was firm, and, unlike Robbie and Martha, she wasn't crying. Opal never cried. She couldn't do that, no matter how sad she was. It was the difference between them.

'You have been a good and faith-filled companion,' she told Garnet in a strong, serious tone that reminded Martha of Uncle Bixbite. 'You have served me loyally and well. You may go proudly.'

Then she held Garnet out towards the Minmangulator.

Martha rushed forward. She couldn't stop herself. She was desperate to touch Garnet one last, last time. Robbie dashed after her, wanting to do the same.

Gently, Opal lifted their hands away. 'Only twenty-three heartbeats left, Earth dwellers,' she whispered, 'so we'd better make it snippy.' She looked down at Garnet. 'Goodbye, my loyal, flying friend.'

She raised her eyes to the ceiling and chanted, '*Bespaxalova cadantzzel beathorow.*' The strange words sounded like a prayer. Once she had finished speaking them, Opal slotted Garnet's body into the opening at the top of the Minmangulator.

She let him go.

There was no bump, as Martha expected, no sound of him dropping to the floor. All she could hear was Robbie sniffing, the rain showering down outside and her own tears pattering onto the floor.

The little swing door at the opening of the silver cube flicked silently to and fro like a flap on a letterbox, and then fell still.

Keeping their eyes fixed on the Minmangulator, Robbie and Martha stepped back and joined Opal, who took their hands in hers. No one spoke. They all stood, deep in their thoughts, as the rain cascaded down on the parachute silk above them.

Martha wrapped her cloak around her. It had warmed and dried her at once; even her fingers had warmed up. Opal's hand, though, resting in her own, felt as cold as an ice cube. Her face had turned a strange colour, too. It was so pale it was almost transparent, and it was getting visibly thinner. Her cheekbones still stood out strongly but her cheeks were caving inwards beneath them. She looked as though all the life was draining out of her.

Which, Martha suddenly realised, was exactly what was happening.

'Opal!' she shouted. 'You haven't got a mingle. You have to make another one. You have to use the Minmangulator now. Quickly! Hurry!'

'Dear Garnie,' Opal murmured. 'Quite the best mingle I ever managed.'

'Opal! Be quick!' Martha was desperate. If Opal didn't act quickly, they would have put Garnet in the Minmangulator for nothing. 'Opal! Switch it on!'

Opal looked at her, her eyes a very pale violet. She hardly seemed to recognise Martha, and she didn't look as if she had the energy to do anything at all. She had been so confident and strong, but now she was collapsing, unable to do what she was supposed to do, unable even to remember what she was supposed to do.

Martha realised that if Opal couldn't act, she was going to have to act for her. She hadn't been able to save Garnet, but she was going to save Opal. She would do whatever it took.

She rushed to the Minmangulator and searched for a way to turn it on. There were no buttons or switches that she could see. She ran her hands over every surface but couldn't find anything. She had a horrible feeling that Opal had once told her that they didn't use switches on Carnelia.

'Maybe there's a remote control,' said Robbie, wiping away tears as he saw what the problem was. He jumped up and down in front of Opal, trying to get her attention. 'Where's the remote, Opal? Where's the remote?'

'I'm the remote,' said Opal, smiling faintly. She was speaking much too dreamily for Martha's liking. She remembered now that everything the Moonbabies used was powered not by controls, but by their eyes. Only Opal could operate the Minmangulator. Right now she didn't look as if she could operate a pencil sharpener.

Martha went to her and patted her shrinking cheek. It wasn't too late; it couldn't be too late, she wouldn't let it be.

'Come on, Opal,' she said, patting and patting. 'This is urgent. You have to hold on. You have to make the Minmangulator work. You have to do it now!'

'What's wrong with her?' said Robbie. 'Why isn't she doing anything?'

'I don't know,' said Martha, determined not to panic despite the fact that Opal was starting to shudder and shake. 'She can't hear me for some reason. Opal!'

Suddenly it seemed as if their fantastic summer, their wonderful year together, was about to end in the most awful way imaginable. Martha cried out without even knowing she was going to: 'I will not let this happen! I will not!'

She pulled Opal's head downwards, forcing her to meet her gaze.

'Wake up, Opal! You can't live without a mingle. You have to make one now!' Opal's violet eyes were alarmingly empty of either expression or understanding. 'Come *on*!' Martha hissed. 'You can't give up now! Uncle Bixbite doesn't want to lose you. Carnelia doesn't want to lose you. *I* don't want to lose you! You're my best friend in the universe, Opal Moonbaby. You're my star sister, remember. Now wake up and switch on that machine!'

At those words, Opal's vacant expression disappeared at last, and she focused properly on Martha. Her eyes looked sickly and wan, but her pupils were shining. 'You're not going to lose me, Martha,' she whispered. 'Never. Not once in a blue lagoon!' Then she closed her eyes. Martha thought she had gone to sleep or, worse, fallen unconscious.

'Opal!' she cried. 'Opal! Where are you? Where have you gone? Come back!'

'It's all right, Martha,' said Robbie from behind her. 'It's all right. She's doing it. Look!'

Martha turned to see the entire Minmangulator lit up with an eerie lilac light. Purple patterns swirled all over it; they moved quickly around and around the glowing cube, as if they were chasing one another.

The Minmangulator was working!

'He's going,' Martha said, not quite believing her eyes but knowing it was true.

She suddenly had an overwhelming desire to give Garnet something. Some kind of leaving present. Impulsively, she picked up a few of his favourite cat biscuits. Garnet probably wouldn't be able to eat them, wherever he was going, but at least he would have them with him. She stepped forward and lifted the flap on the Minmangulator. She looked back at Opal. She wasn't sure if what she was doing was allowed.

Opal's eyes were open again. She nodded, and Martha posted the handful of biscuits through the flap. They weren't much, but they were better than nothing.

'I want to give him something too.' Robbie pulled a long feather from under his t-shirt. 'It's the biggest one I've found all holiday. Could even have been a record-breaker, but I want Garnie to have it.' He stepped forward, but instead of putting the feather through the flap as Martha had done, he started to poke it down the cylindrical hole on top of the Minmangulator, the one that looked like a chimney.

'No,' said Opal faintly. 'Don't put it in the expulsion vent or you'll—'

The feather disappeared.

'—interrupt the minmangulating process,' Opal finished.

The patterns stopped moving and there was an ugly sound of grinding and chopping. Splinters of feather flew out of the chimney hole. The Minmangulator flashed red and started to hum loudly. A sharp burning smell filled the Domestipod.

'Oh, Robbie!' Martha cried. 'What have you done?'

Robbie's hands flew to his mouth. 'I'm sorry! I'm sorry! I didn't mean to!'

'What's happening, Opal?' said Martha. 'Is it broken?'

Opal shook her head. 'I don't know. This has never happened before. I think it's stuck.'

'It can't be! You need a mingle! It has to work. It has to!'

Martha couldn't believe it. They were so close to getting a new mingle. It had been so hard to put Garnet in the machine, so painful, but they had done it. Now it felt as if Garnet had gone in there for nothing, as if all their work was wasted.

'I jammed it!' Robbie wailed. 'I'm so sorry!'

They all stared at the flashing machine, willing it to work. The flashing continued and the humming became louder and more urgent.

'Please,' Martha whispered. 'Please, please, please.'

Eventually the flashes became fewer and further between and the humming slowed to a gentle whirr. Patterns swirled across the sides of the Minmangulator again. Not just patterns now, but pictures too. Pictures of ears, of whiskers and fins. Pictures of claws and eyes and fur. A catalogue of animal parts, ready for picking. Opal blinked from time to time as if she was choosing a part for her new mingle. That made Martha think things were going to be OK. She allowed herself a small shaky sigh.

At last the pictures stopped whirling and faded away. The Minmangulator went back to being a silver cube.

Everything went silent. Even the rain had stopped falling. A yellowish glow lit up the Domestipod. Martha had a vague realisation that, outside, the sun must have come out. But that was outside. Anything that was happening out there had nothing to do with them.

Thud-ud.

Martha jumped. Inside the Minmangulator, something had dropped to the floor. But what?

✺ ✹ ✺

There was a click, and the whole front of the Minmangulator fell open and stood ajar, like a door.

Martha held her breath. Something was lying on a shelf at the bottom of the Minmangulator. Whatever it was, was lying very still.

Too still.

'What is that?' Robbie bit at his thumbnail as he stared at the motionless pile of fur. 'Is it a new mingle? Is it . . . is it—'

'Is it alive?' Martha finished.

Opal didn't answer her. With great effort, she widened her eyes and whispered, '*Chadanzzequet.*'

The door of the Minmàngulator swung wider and the pile of fur moved. Martha almost cried out with relief. It seemed a new mingle had been made after all.

A new mingle had been made, and it was living.

That meant Opal would survive.

At first Martha looked away. She didn't want to meet Garnet's replacement. It was too soon. The thought of it gave her a pain in her chest. She couldn't look at this new mixed-up animal, whatever it was, not when in her heart she was still saying goodbye to Garnet.

Chi-chi.

Hearing that small sound, curiosity got the better of her. Martha looked, after all, just in time to see the new mingle stand a little unsteadily on its short legs. She saw it open its wide, round eyes and stretch its blue-grey wings. She saw it stagger forward and then fly out of the Minmangulator and up into the air. It flew round and round their heads, crying *chiwee-chiwee-chiwee.* Then it landed in Opal Moonbaby's spiky hair. It sat with its wings outspread, kneading her scalp and purring. The feel of it there seemed to restore Opal to herself at once. She looked up at the creature and laughed.

187

'Well, you arrived just in the nick-nack of time, didn't you?!'

Chigga-chigga-chigga, the creature replied, shaking its wings a little, like a newly hatched butterfly drying out in the sun.

This was so weird, Martha thought. She could have sworn the animal looked exactly like . . . but that wasn't possible. What was going on? Confused, she gazed at Robbie, who gazed back at her with the same dumbstruck expression she knew was on her own face. She knew they were both thinking exactly the same thing, but neither of them wanted to be the first to say it.

Robbie licked his lips. 'But that's . . . that's not a new . . . that's not. Isn't that . . .?'

He couldn't bring himself to say the word, so Martha said it for him.

'Isn't that . . . Garnet?'

Opal chuckled. 'I do believe,' she said, reaching up and tickling the animal under its chin, 'that it *is* him. It's the spiffing image of him! It is him in almost every way.'

'You mean, he didn't get re-minmangulated?' said Martha, hardly daring to believe her eyes, or her ears. 'He hasn't been recycled?'

'No, he hasn't. I think something else has occurred here. Something new. If you ask me, Garnet has not been recycled in the usual way. He's been rubbed up and brushed down a little, but he hasn't been recycled. He's simply been *refreshed*!' Opal turned to Robbie. 'Thanks to you, Cucumber Hero.'

'I did it?' said Robbie.

'Indeed you did. You have discovered a whole new use for the Minmangulator. *Mingle-refreshing*. I can see that catching on. I can see it becoming a whole new craze. From now on, if Carnelians want to keep their mingles, they'll be able to. They'll do it by putting a feather in the expulsion vent, just like you did. The Robbie Stephens Feather Way! In my opinion, Robbie, you should be given a Carnelian Award for Ingenuity and Geniusness!'

'Wow,' said Robbie. He puffed out his chest. 'That would be well slick!'

'It's really, really him,' said Martha, patting Garnet's little head. She patted him all over, still needing to make absolutely sure it was him. Everything was in order: his wings were in the right place, his lynx tail and ears too. His stoat's nose was pink and moist, and his Persian cat fur was gorgeously glossy. His owl's amber eyes were bright again, bright with all the intelligence of a pot-bellied pig.

Martha laughed with joy. 'He looks just like new!'

'He is new,' said Opal. 'In almost every way. He's a bit younger, perhaps, but the wonderful thing is, he's still the same old Garnie.' She slapped her thigh. 'Darn it, Garnet! You're still the cutest and most splendid mingle I ever managed!'

Chigga-chigga, said Garnet, revolving his head in agreement.

'Chigga-chigga to you, Garnie,' said Robbie. He joined Martha and they stroked and stroked and stroked the mingle just where he sat, in his all-time favourite place, on Opal Moonbaby's head.

M um hopped out of the car to close the gate. Martha rolled down her window and inhaled deeply. The campsite smelt green and fresh and salty. She knew that smell would always remind her of their holiday in Stormhaven.

'It is a bit odd though, isn't it?' Mum said, hopping back in again and fastening her seatbelt. 'Opal's uncle coming to collect her in the middle of the night, taking the tent down in the dark. He could at least have come and said goodbye.'

Sam looked both ways before pulling out into the winding lane. 'Probably didn't want to wake you.'

'All the same,' said Mum. 'I think it's peculiar.'

'That's astronauts for you, I guess.' Sam shrugged. 'A breed apart.'

'Bixbite's that, all right.' Mum switched on the radio and began to sing along to the tune that came on. Sam joined in.

Robbie was spinning Yoyo round and round in his hands. 'Aw, put something else on, will you? That song sounds like it's from the Ice Age. Is that when you two were young?'

'Don't be so cheeky!' said Mum, but she laughed.

Sam laughed too. And they kept on singing.

Martha took one last look back at the campsite, at the farmer's dog that stood scratching itself by the gate, at the yellow patches the tent and the Domestipod had left behind on the grass. Patches that would soon be green again, as if none of them had ever been there.

But they had.

Martha rested her head on the cool box and curled herself into a ball. She was tired now, but in a nice way. She felt warm and cosy, like a contented cat basking in the sunshine. She hadn't slept much during the night. She had been far too excited to do anything as normal as sleeping.

Because the previous evening, while they had been lying in the field, watching Garnet chasing dragonflies, Opal had told Martha the most amazing news. She'd announced that she wasn't going to go back to Carnelia after all. She said she'd decided to stay on Earth instead.

Martha hadn't believed her at first. Even after

Opal assured her that it wasn't a joke, that she'd never been more serious about anything in her life, Martha had been too stunned to take it in. She couldn't understand how Opal would suddenly give up her CIA, her chance to be Queen of Carnelia, her entire future!

Opal's eyes had danced and sparkled as she explained. 'I nearly lost Garnet in the Minmangulator today,' she said, 'and I nearly lost you in the ocean. I'm not going to let that happen again. You're my Best Friend in the Universe, Martha, and I'm never going to be parted from you. I'm staying with you on Earth now, for good and ever.'

'Are you sure?' Martha was thrilled by the idea, but she was worried Opal might be being hasty. 'What about your CIA, what about Uncle Bixbite?'

'I don't care two honks for my CIA,' Opal answered. 'Not any more. And I'm sure Uncle Bixbite will be able to find another Moonbaby to be Carnelian Coronet-holder eventually. I've got some Moonbaby cousins coming along. They may only be little waddlers at the moment – most of them are only knee-high to a space-hopper – but I'm sure they'll make better Coronet-holders than I ever would. They'll be much more logical than I'd be now.'

She had pulled at the long grass, stripping away the seeds with her fingers. 'The other Moonbabies won't get attached to their mingles like I did, or to their friends. They'll rule the planet in the proper Carnelian way. Logic is king, remember, Martha. That's what we say on Carnelia. Trouble is,' Garnet came up, and she buried her nose in his fresh white fur, 'I don't believe it any more.'

'You're sure?' Martha still hardly dared to believe what she was hearing. 'You're sure you want to stay?'

'It's what you want too, isn't it, Martha?' Opal had looked deep into her eyes. 'You want me to stay?'

Martha had never said it out loud, but there was nothing in the world she wanted more. It was her greatest wish.

Opal tossed the grass seed high into the air. 'That's settled, then,' she said as the seed landed on their heads like confetti. 'I'm staying on Earth for good, and we'll be best friends together forever.'

Then she and Martha had both jumped up, grabbed one another's hands and danced round and round the yellow-coated Domestipod, singing, 'Best friends together forever, best friends together forever,' until they were completely out of breath.

At bedtime, Martha had gone back to the tent. She had made herself a space among the burst footballs, wriggled into her sleeping bag and told Robbie about Opal's decision to stay on Earth.

'Awesome,' Robbie had said as he fell asleep. It was funny how easily he'd accepted the news. Martha's thoughts were in a total whirl, and she'd lain awake long into the night. Some time in the early hours, well before dawn, a gentle breeze had rippled the walls of the tent and she had known that the Domestipod was lifting away from the field and setting off for the Half Moon Estate.

It would only be a few hours before she saw Opal again. She would be able to see her all the time from now on, every single day. So she didn't mind waiting. She had always assumed that she would have to say goodbye to Opal one day, but it wasn't going to be like that now. Now they could stay together forever.

Martha hugged herself and gazed up at the blue sky. She loved the way the clouds went dashing past. She loved the music Mum had put on the radio. She loved Mum. She loved Robbie. She didn't love Sam, of course, but she wasn't cross with him any longer. She wasn't sorry he'd brought them to Stormhaven, either. People who went on cruises and safaris called them 'holidays of a lifetime'. Well, she felt as if she'd been on a holiday of a lifetime, too. It was a holiday in which mingles had been refreshed for the first time ever, a holiday in which lives had been saved, decisions made and friendships deepened.

She couldn't imagine having another holiday like it in her whole entire life.

The feeling she had now was the best feeling possible; it was like being a character at the end of a really happy film. Even Mum and Sam's singing seemed to fit in with her happiness. It was the soundtrack to the film, the closing music playing as the credits rolled. She shut her eyes and smiled as she felt herself drifting off into a delicious sleep.

✶ ✶ ✶

'Only if it's all right with you two,' Mum was saying when Martha opened her eyes again. 'You have a say too, you know.'

Martha must have nodded off for quite a time, because they were on the motorway now. Mum was driving while Sam snored next to her in the passenger seat.

'Yay,' said Robbie, lobbing Yoyo at the ceiling and catching him. 'It's going to be fantastic!'

'Say in what?' said Martha. 'What's going to be fantastic?'

'I asked Mum if she and Sam are going to move in together,' Robbie told her. 'And they are! Woohoo!'

'That's not exactly what I said, actually,' said Mum. 'We were planning to talk to you about it properly when we got home. But since you've brought it up, Robbie ...' She sighed. 'Anyway, I said it depends on you two. What *you* think.'

'I think it'll be storming!' said Robbie. 'That's my new word, by the way. I got it from the holiday. Stormhaven, storming. Get it?' He used Yoyo to scratch an itch on his nose. 'Hey, if Sam lives with us, does that mean we get free swimming lessons from now on?'

'No, it does not.' Mum sat up straighter, trying to see Martha's face in the rear-view mirror. 'What do you think, Martha?'

This was the very announcement Martha had been dreading, ever since Sam had first started coming round to their flat. But she hadn't thought about him and Mum and their relationship for quite a while; there had been far more pressing things on her mind. She wasn't sure if she felt as strongly about it now.

'We don't have to do anything straight away,' Mum said. 'Not unless you're both happy too.'

Martha stretched and yawned. She looked over at Sam snoozing in the passenger seat, the side of his head pressed into the headrest. She was sort of used to him now. Without him they would never have gone to Stormhaven. She hadn't wanted to go, but the holiday had turned out brilliantly and now she wouldn't have missed it for anything.

And Sam had been kind to them. He'd shown them loads of things at the beach they would never have found or even known about otherwise; he'd joined in with their games when they needed an extra player and he'd left them alone when they'd wanted to be on their own without any adults.

Lots of the things Sam did had irritated her before, but she realised now that he had only been trying to make friends.

Sam let out a snore. He had a very peculiar way of

snoring. His mouth kept opening at one corner and he puffed air out of it. It made her giggle. She had to admit, Sam was quite funny to have around.

'It's cool,' she said.

'Cool?' Mum sounded uncertain. 'Is that all?'

Martha made a face. 'It's fine. If you and Sam really like each other, you should probably live together. I mean, that's what people do, isn't it? So I think you should. As long as you're sure.'

Mum's eyes crinkled in the mirror. 'Thank you for your advice, Martha. And I am sure. If you're sure, I'm sure too.'

'OK, then.' Martha looked out of the window. She had no idea how they were going to fit Sam into the flat with them, but at this moment she didn't care. She was happy, and she wanted everyone else to be happy too.

'But don't you want to know the details?' Mum said. 'There's a lot to organise. And we've had an idea.'

'You can tell me later if you like.' Martha was watching the clouds rushing through the sky. 'Tell me when you're not driving.' The clouds seemed to be racing the car as if they too were keen to get back to Archwell and Opal.

As they crawled home through the Saturday afternoon traffic, Martha thought Archwell and the Half Moon Estate looked smaller than before.

The estate was Martha's world. Their flat, the mini-market, the park — even school was only down the road. Everything she did, everywhere she went was here, or had been until recently. She had only been away for a fortnight, but so much had happened in that fortnight she felt as if she had been away much, much longer.

She was relieved to spot the Domestipod tucked in behind the trees, back in its usual position on the edge of the park. Now that it was uncovered again, it seemed to stand out more than ever. It struck Martha how very different it was from all the other

houses and flats in the neighbourhood, how purple it was and how shiny.

Even better, Opal was there too. Just as she'd promised she would be. She was lying in the play-pipe with her head sticking out of one end, facing the sky.

Opal turned as they pulled up outside the flats. She slid out of the pipe and came over.

As Opal walked towards them, Martha thought there was something different about her. She couldn't put her finger on what it was exactly, but she seemed to be moving more slowly, more serenely than usual. Garnet, on the other hand, was dashing madly round her legs. He was full of energy since his time in the Minmángulator.

'Been back a while, Opal?' said Mum. 'Good journey home?'

'I had an excellent journey, Marie Stephens, thank you for asking. I got back as quick as blinking.' She winked one violet eye at Martha. Opal's eyes were so beautiful, always dancing about, looking for fun. Martha was probably imagining it, but she thought they seemed a tiny bit more serious than usual. Martha wondered if anything had happened, a row with Uncle Bixbite perhaps, but Opal beamed at her, twinkling reassurance.

'Hiya, hiya!' Alesha was waving at them. She came clattering along in a new pair of bright orange shoes with very high heels. She gave Mum such a big hug she nearly knocked her off the pavement.

'Welcome home, Marie. Ooh, I missed you!' Alesha never normally called Mum 'Marie'. She always called her Mariella, because she thought it sounded more Italian. And she never hugged anybody.

Mum was obviously surprised by her boss's unusually enthusiastic welcome. She struggled to keep her balance and then hugged Alesha back. 'Hi. How was Italy?'

Alesha wrinkled her nose. 'Oh, it was OK. But it's not all it's cracked up to be. The heat didn't suit me. Or the food. You can't get a decent peanut-butter sandwich *anywhere*. They do have nice shoes, though.' She lifted a foot, criss-crossed with tiny orange leather straps. Her toes peeped out of the ends, complete with orange nail varnish.

'I don't know why I ever thought I'd want to live there. Who wants to live in a sauna? They can keep their cappuccinos and their polenta casseroles. Give me a nice hot chocolate and a buttered teacake any day. No. Archwell's my manor, always has been.'

Martha grinned at Opal, but she didn't seem to be listening to Alesha. She looked dreamy and distant. Martha was just about to ask her what was on her mind when Jessie appeared.

'Hi, Martha. Hi, Opal. Hi, Robbie,' she said. 'How was your holiday? Did you have a good time?'

'Oh, hi!' Martha gave Jessie a hug. She was really

pleased to see her. It was quite a clumsy hug because of the elbow pads Jessie was wearing and the skateboard she was carrying.

'The holiday was brilliant, thanks,' Martha said. 'Actually it was . . . amazing!' She couldn't say more, but it didn't matter because Jessie was full of her own news.

'Great. Gran and I had a fab holiday too. I hated the plane journey, but it was worth it. I saw a turtle! When did you get back? Have you been in the new skateboard bowl yet?'

Martha shook her head. So much had happened in Stormhaven, she had forgotten all about the skateboard bowl.

'You've got to see it! We raised enough money at the Fun Fete and now it's finished. Come and have a look. It's awesome!'

'This is going to be extreme!' Robbie said, already racing ahead of them. 'I'm on my storming way!'

'Hey!' Mum called. 'What about unloading the car?'

'That's OK,' said Sam. 'I'll take care of it, Marie. Go and have a cup of tea with Alesha, and you kids can go and skate your brains out!'

Martha gave Sam a grateful smile. 'Come and have a go later, if you like,' she said, and she and Opal and Jessie ran after Robbie.

The skateboard bowl looked completely different. It had been a real mess when they had left Archwell, but now it was perfectly smooth and grey. It looked like a stone washbasin belonging to a giant.

They all took turns on Jessie's skateboard. It was hard to balance, and Martha, Jessie and Robbie fell off loads of times. Opal didn't have any problems. She swept up and down the bowl twenty times or so, doing flips and tricks as if she'd been skateboarding all her life.

'Rock 'n' rule!' she said, raising a fist in the air as she finished her tenth circuit. She didn't seem very triumphant, though. Not the way she had been on the Bucking Bronco at the Fun Fete. She handed the skateboard to Martha, and left the bowl and went off to sit on one of the park benches. She sat with her ankles crossed and her hands in her lap, staring up at the trees.

Martha would have liked another go on the skateboard, but she gave her turn to Jessie and went to sit next to Opal.

Opal kept staring at the branches above them. Some of the leaves were already starting to turn yellow. Martha wasn't sure what to say. She'd never seen Opal in this mood before. She didn't know what it could mean.

'You're really good at skateboarding,' she tried at last.

Opal smiled.

'Must be all that asteroid-riding you do on Carnelia.'

'Used to do,' Opal corrected her.

'Used to do, then,' said Martha.

A leaf fluttered down in front of them. They both watched as Garnet jumped at it and then tore it up with his tiny teeth, growling at the leaf as if it was alive.

'Uncle Bixbite's coming in a few days, isn't he?' said Martha. 'For your Final Ascendance.'

'He is.' Opal leant forward and stroked Garnet's head.

'What will he say when you tell him you're not going back?'

Opal sighed. 'Poor Uncle Bixie! He'll throw a mammoth woolly wobbly, no doubt about it. Never mind. He won't have a totally wasted journey. He won't get me, of course, or the Full and Final Earth Report he's expecting, but I'll still be able to give him this.'

She took the *Human Handybook* from her back pocket and flicked through its well-thumbed pages, all of them covered in her jagged handwriting. 'There's an entire year's Earth research in here.'

'Is that what's bothering you?' Martha asked. 'Telling Uncle Bixbite?' She thought that must be it. Opal had been so happy in Stormhaven, and that was only one day ago. Nothing had changed since then, so there couldn't be any other problem, could there?

'I'm not getting chilly toes, if that's what's worrying you,' Opal said.

'Cold feet,' said Martha. 'And I was wondering.'

'No.' Opal took Martha's hand in hers. 'I promised you last night I would stay on Earth, didn't I? And I will. I'll explain it all to Uncle Bixie as soon as he gets here. I'll stick to my gums, you'll see.'

Opal held on to Martha's hands for a bit longer and then said, 'Although it'll be a lot easier if you're there too, when he does come. You will be with me, won't you? You won't let me face his music on my own?'

Martha swallowed. She didn't really fancy being around when Opal broke the news to her uncle that she didn't care about her CIA, that she wasn't going back to Carnelia and would never ever be the Carnelian Coronet-holder. She would much prefer to stay in bed with her head under the pillow until she was sure he was safely back on his planet. But she wanted Opal to relax and be happy again.

'Of course I'll be with you,' she said. 'That's what friends are for.'

'Yes,' said Opal. 'That's it. We'll do everything together now, won't we, Martha? We'll just be a couple of human friends who do everything together.'

'Yes,' Martha said contentedly. 'We will.' She linked arms with Opal and they looked out over the park together. They didn't need to say anything, because they knew everything that was in each other's minds.

Chi-chi-chi-cha!

Garnet, who had been rolling around playing with the leaf, suddenly sat bolt upright, his ears raised and sharp. He flared his stoat's nostrils and whined.

'Oh, look!' Martha pointed across the park. 'It's Mrs Underedge and Bonnie-Belle-Flower-Lady! I think they're going for a run!'

It wasn't exactly running Mrs Underedge was doing. It wasn't even jogging. It was more a sort of twisty speed-walking, which made her hips shift forwards and backwards as she moved. She was wearing very white trainers that looked brand new, and she had her suit trousers clipped in round her ankles.

Bonnie-Belle-Flower-Lady was lagging behind, and Mrs Underedge kept having to stop and tug at her lead.

Chi-chi chagga-chi! Garnet jumped up in the air, all four legs leaving the ground at once, and dashed towards them.

'He's running to see his girlfriend,' said Martha. 'He must have been really missing her.'

Bonnie-Belle-Flower-Lady didn't try to run. She waddled along behind Mrs Underedge. She didn't seem to have spotted Garnet.

'Hello, girls,' puffed Mrs Underedge, stopping to prop her glasses up on her nose. 'Have you been having a good holiday?'

'Yes, thank you,' Martha replied. 'How's Bonnie-Belle-Flower-Lady?' She watched Garnet jump around the little dog. He was licking and sniffing her, trying to attract her attention again, but Bonnie-Belle-Flower-Lady wasn't even looking at Garnet. She was gazing over her shoulder, as if she'd like to go home.

'She's a worry to me, as a matter of fact,' said Mrs Underedge, frowning down at her pet. 'She's become a trifle plump lately, and rather lazy about her walkies. That's why I've invested in these sports shoes. We could both do with being a little fitter. As of today, I'm cutting down on her Good Girl biscuits and starting a whole new exercise regime.'

Opal was staring at Bonnie-Belle-Flower-Lady, who was still ignoring Garnet's advances. 'You should look after that dog, Mrs U,' she said suddenly. 'She's more delicate than you think.'

Mrs Underedge was taken aback. 'Thank you, Opal. I intend to look after her. Nothing but the best for my Bonnie-Belle-Flower-Lady.' She pulled the lead a little tighter, pulling Bonnie-Belle-Flower-Lady away from Garnet, who was still sniffing enthusiastically. 'Well, I must be getting along. We have three circuits of the park to do yet.' She paused. 'By the way, Opal, do you still have my parachute silk?'

'Yes, I've got it,' said Opal. 'It's all safe and soundproof.'

'Excellent, I'll call in for it. What day would be convenient?'

'Any day's convenient for me,' said Opal. 'I'm not going anywhere. I'll be here forever now, won't I, Martha?'

Martha grinned as Opal winked at her.

Garnet gave up trying to get Bonnie-Belle-Flower-Lady to notice him and went back to nibbling at his leaf. Mrs Underedge seemed rather satisfied about that.

'What about Saturday?' she said. 'I'll call for the parachute on Saturday.' She bent to retie one of her laces and then stood up and flexed her feet one at a time. 'I am looking forward to next term, girls. I have some really tricky quadratic equations lined up for you. And we've a brand new topic. Animals in their natural habitats. Won't that be fun!'

'Cool,' said Martha. She didn't know if she'd enjoy doing quadratic equations, but she loved finding out about animals and the places they lived. It was one of her favourite things.

'Cool,' echoed Opal. 'Can't wait.' She didn't sound all that excited, though. Maybe even Opal had got used to school, Martha thought; it couldn't be quite as thrilling for her now as when she had first gone there nearly a year before.

Mrs Underedge was warming up to do her twisty walk again. 'Well, goodbye,' she said, and she went swivelling away, dragging Bonnie-Belle-Flower-Lady behind her.

Garnet stopped nibbling his leaf and looked after

them mournfully. Martha beckoned to him. He sprang onto her lap and whimpered.

'What's got into Bonnie-Belle-Flower-Lady, eh?' Martha stroked him. 'Why didn't she want to play today?'

'Garnet's too young for her now,' said Opal. 'Since he's been refreshed he looks just like a puppy to her, or a kitten. And anyway,' she watched the dog trotting reluctantly behind her mistress, 'I think Bonnie-Belle-Flower-Lady's got other things on her mind these days. I don't think she's feeling very playful.'

Martha laughed. 'No, she's a proper grown-up lady now, isn't she?' She scratched Garnet's nose. 'Too posh for you, Garnie. Never mind, we'll still play with you.'

Chi-cha! Garnet nuzzled her and then pricked up his ears as Robbie shouted, 'Hey Garnie, come over here. I'll give you a ride on the skateboard!'

Bonnie-Belle-Flower-Lady wasn't the only one not feeling playful. Opal didn't seem very playful either.

'What do you want to do?' Martha said, bursting into the Domestipod on their third morning back. 'Do you want to play Hide and Seek, or go to the end of the road and back? Or do you want to chase bikes?' She had rescued her Summer Schedule of Stuff To Do from her desk. They didn't really need it now that Opal was staying for good. There was no hurry to do any of the activities, but she thought it might still be fun to do them.

To her surprise, Opal was lying in her hammock. It wasn't like her to sleep in in the mornings.

'You decide,' Opal said, leaning out of the

hammock and reading the list over Martha's shoulder. 'Which one do you want to do, Martha?'

Martha didn't want to decide. She wanted Opal to jump down from the hammock, seize the list from her and demand to do all of the activities at once. That's what she would have done this time last year. Martha was pretty sure she would have done that a few days ago, too.

'I dunno.' Martha shrugged. 'Maybe we'll just hang out on the play-pipe.'

'All right,' said Opal. 'Pipe it is.'

She swung her legs over the side of the hammock and let herself gently down to the floor. Normally Opal would have somersaulted out of the hammock and bounced around, eager to get the fun started.

Martha didn't know what was wrong. She knew Opal was anxious about Uncle Bixbite's arrival on Ascendance Day, but she was sure there was more to it than that. She found herself wishing for the zillionth time that she could read minds the way Opal could.

'You don't need to do that,' Opal said. 'I've told you everything I'm thinking. Honestly I have.'

'Honestly?'

'Honestly and truly and yours most sincerely,' Opal said. The words were reassuring but her voice sounded flat.

Martha felt a bit flat herself. The blissful end-of-the-film feeling she had had in the car on the way home had faded. She ought to be feeling brilliant. Garnet had been saved and refreshed, and Opal had decided to stay on Earth so they would be together forever. She should have been as happy and carefree as a bird gliding around in the sky, but it wasn't like that, somehow. Martha could tell, whatever Opal said, that she wasn't happy. And if Opal wasn't happy, she couldn't be either.

Opal's eyes had lost a little of their vivid brightness, her shoulders slumped down in a way they never had before, and she would often break off from what they were doing or stop speaking in the middle of a sentence and stare hard for ages at nothing at all.

At first Martha thought she might be tired after all the excitement at Stormhaven, but when she asked her, Opal said she wasn't tired. She said she was as fit as a fiddle-faddle. Nevertheless, her eyes continued to fade. Her face started to look a little grey, and her hair, normally so tall and proud on her head, began to wilt and flop around her pointed ears.

Martha knew Opal wasn't deliberately keeping anything from her. She trusted her absolutely. If she said she wasn't keeping any secrets, then she wasn't.

But there was definitely a problem, and Martha was determined to figure out what it was.

✦ ✤ ✦

'It was nothing,' Robbie burbled in his sleep. 'Just ingenuity and geniusness, really. Thanks very much.'

215

He was lying below Martha on the bottom bunk. Martha could tell he was having a lovely dream. He was accepting his Carnelian Award for Ingenuity and Geniusness.

She wished she could be asleep, too. She'd been awake for hours trying to imagine what it would be like when Uncle Bixbite arrived the next day, and wondering just how angry he was going to be.

And it was such a big decision Opal had made. After tomorrow, there would be no going back on it, ever. Opal was probably the only alien who had ever decided to stay on Earth for their whole life. Even though she wanted her to stay, more than anything, Martha couldn't help wondering if her friend had made the right choice. Opal's hair had continued to wilt over the last few days until it had dropped down completely. Now it was as dull and as flat as a human's. Martha could tell Opal wasn't herself, but she couldn't work out why.

At last Martha gave up trying to go to sleep and got out of bed. She picked her way through a maze of Robbie's burst footballs and went to the bathroom to get a drink of water. She was on the way back to bed when something made her stop and go to the window. She drew back the curtain a little and peeped outside.

It was very dark, but in the soft, orangey glow of the street lamp that lit the entrance to the park, Martha saw Opal. She was lying on her back on the Domestipod roof and she was staring hard at the sky, as if she was straining to see something far, far away. Martha guessed she was trying to see Carnelia.

After a while, Opal stopped peering at the sky and began to pace about on the roof of her little house. She covered the whole roof in three quick strides. One two three, one two three, backwards and forwards she went, faster and faster. She reminded Martha of the tiger she had seen when Sam had taken them to the zoo at the start of the summer holiday. It had roamed around like that too, brushing its long body against the transparent walls of its cage. Martha had felt sorry for the tiger. She was sure it was remembering the sights and smells of the jungle where it had been born. Where it had been taken from. Where it belonged.

Animals in their natural habitats.

Suddenly Martha knew exactly what was wrong.

She pinched the material of the curtain between her fingers and thought about Opal's future on Earth. She thought about what lay ahead for her friend. She imagined her sitting hunched on the small school chairs, doing algebra and spelling, learning about animals in their natural habitats. She'd have to go to secondary school after that, and then she'd have to get a job. What kind of job, Martha wondered? Mum still sometimes skimmed an eye over the *Situations Vacant* column in the local newspaper, but the jobs in there were all for supermarket cashiers or personal assistants or gardeners. Martha couldn't imagine Opal doing any of those jobs. But what would she do? There were no vacancies for trainee planet rulers, or people with amazing eye power; there was nothing like that in the *Archwell Gazette*.

To her relief, Opal stopped pacing eventually and sat down. She hugged her legs to her and used her wonderful, powerful eyes to look no further than the tops of her own knees.

Martha let the curtain drop. She drank her water and got back into bed.

Opal had been telling the truth when she had promised she wasn't keeping a secret, Martha was quite convinced of that. But she knew now, thanks to Opal, that there was another type of secret, the type of secret you buried so far down inside you that you kept it even from yourself. Opal had found out Martha's secret worry about Sam by looking deep into her mind, deeper than Martha had been prepared to look herself.

Now Martha had seen Opal's secret, she was quite sure of it. It was a relief to know what was wrong at last, but it was a shock too.

The question was, what should she do about it?

It's time I made a decision, Martha thought as she got back under the covers. She lay awake even longer, planning and plotting into the night. The more she thought about it, the more she knew that what she had decided was right. She also knew that she would never have to make a more difficult decision than this one in her entire life.

'What?' Opal cried. '*Why* can't you hang out with me this morning?' She looked quite lost when Martha broke the news. She kicked her feet against the concrete pipe. 'We're sticking together like gum trees from now on, remember. That's why I'm staying on Earth. So we can be with each other all the time.'

Martha had known Opal would protest. In fact, when morning had come she had thought about going back on her decision. It all seemed much less straightforward in daylight, but whenever she thought of Opal pacing on the roof like that tiger she was convinced that what she was doing was right.

'I know we said we'd be together. But I'm too busy today.'

'Busy doing what? Why do you need to be on your own?' Opal searched Martha's face with her eyes, trying to read her thoughts, but Martha was ready for that and concentrated extremely hard on her own shoes. She focused on her laces. They had lost their plastic tops and were so frayed they were almost impossible to thread. She thought *shoes shoes shoes, laces laces laces* over and over again to stop Opal from seeing what she was really thinking, what she was about to do. She didn't want Opal putting her off.

'Putting you off *what*?' Opal wailed. 'What are you hiding from me, Martha? What?' She seemed almost panicky. It made Martha feel panicky too, but she wasn't about to show it. She put her hands on Opal's shoulders to try and calm her.

'I can't tell you. Not yet. But it's nothing to worry about. Honestly.'

Opal huffed and puffed. She didn't look convinced.

'When we were on the cliff,' Martha said, 'you told me you'd always trust me, remember?'

Opal nodded reluctantly.

'Well, you need to trust me now. Can you do that, do you think? It's all for the best, Opal. Really it is.'

'Promise?'

'Promise. And I promise I'll be there when Uncle Bixbite arrives, too. What time are you expecting him?'

'At the midpoint of your daytime,' said Opal miserably.

222

'That's when I'll come back, then.'

Opal sighed. 'He's expecting my Full and Final Earth Report. I don't know what he's going to say when I tell him I haven't written one. He'll probably fry off the candle!' She pulled her cloak around her, although it wasn't cold. Martha helped her close the edges of the material together.

'What will you do? While I'm away?'

'I won't do anything!' Opal grumbled. 'I'll stay in the Domestipod. I'm going to sit in the shower cubicle with the doors closed and eat popcorn until you come back.'

She dropped down from the pipe, squished Garnet into her pocket and slouched away. Martha hoped Opal wouldn't be angry when she found out what was going on. She couldn't let her thoughts go there, though. She had far too much to do.

'You've hurt her feelings,' said Robbie. Martha had made him stand by the entrance to the flats while she talked to Opal. He had his telescope with him and he was keeping it trained on the Domestipod. 'Maybe I should go and cheer her up.'

'You can't,' said Martha. 'You'd give the game away.' She had sworn Robbie to secrecy, but that wasn't enough. She had to keep him away from Opal. She would definitely see the plan in Robbie's thoughts. Robbie hadn't been keen on the plan at all when she told him about it. She had had a hard job convincing him to go along with it.

'I think you're being cruel,' Robbie said. 'Poor old Opal. She's lonely.'

Martha ignored him. She wasn't being cruel. Or if she was, it was only to be kind.

'You'd better be right about this, Martha,' Robbie warned. 'It's a very storming extreme step you're taking.'

'I know,' said Martha. 'Now come on. We haven't got long.'

They ran all the way to the mini-market. The change that Martha had emptied out of her piggy bank jingled in her pocket. Robbie hurried off down one aisle while Martha spun a display stand round until she found what she was looking for.

They checked out fast and ran to the park and then the play area, collecting all the things on Martha's list. Then they hurried back up to the flat, emptied some toys out of an old shoe box and put everything in there.

Martha brushed a couple of footballs off her chair and sat down at her desk, while Robbie took up his post by the window with his telescope.

'Remember what you have to do,' Martha said as she rummaged in her desk drawer, looking for some paper to write on.

'I know,' said Robbie. 'Keep watch for Uncle Bixbite and tell you the minute he gets here.'

'Good,' said Martha. 'Don't take your eyes off the ball, not even for a second!'

'Aye, aye, Cap'n,' Robbie said in a growly voice. He threw Yoyo up in the air and caught him again. 'If you need us, the cabin boy and me'll be in the crow's nest.' He claimed to have grown out of pirates but he still sometimes liked to pretend he was one. Which was handy, Martha thought, especially today.

There was no paper in the drawer; the only thing in there was the calendar. Martha decided to use that. She ripped out January's picture, turned it over and began to write. It was difficult at first, but once she got going the words sped across the page.

It only seemed about five minutes later when Robbie announced, 'Ahoy there! He's just landed!'

The time had flown by. Martha had filled the backs of January, February and March with writing. Her hand ached like mad, but she had finished. She folded the papers, stashed them in her pocket and joined Robbie at the window.

'Martha!' he said. 'You'd better prepare to walk the plank!'

Uncle Bixbite's silver, egg-shaped spaceship was parked neatly in among the giant bins outside the flats. It was a little taller and a little shinier than the other bins, but you'd never notice it was there. Not unless you knew what you were looking for.

Uncle Bixbite was already striding towards the Domestipod.

'Quick!' said Martha. 'Let's get down there now. Opal needs us!'

Opal had been true to her word. She was sitting in the shower cubicle, fully clothed, with her cloak draped over her and some popcorn scattered around the shower tray. The shower doors, which still had Martha's name scrawled all over them, were closed and Uncle Bixbite was struggling to see between all the letters. He was trying to get a proper look at Garnet, who was cowering slightly on Opal's shoulder.

'And you haven't re-minmangulated yet,' he said, as his own terrapin mingle looked on, its sharp squirrel eyes glittering with disapproval. 'You haven't packed your things, or secured your furniture for the flight home. What in the name of Carnelia is going on?'

Opal didn't answer. Uncle Bixbite threw up his arms in exasperation. Neither of them seemed to notice Martha and Robbie standing in the doorway.

'This is Ascendance Day,' Uncle Bixbite exclaimed. 'I was looking forward to giving you your Carnelian Independence Award, but now I don't know if you deserve it. I can't think what you're playing at, Opal.' He peered at her flat hair drawn back into a limp ponytail. 'Are you unwell? Have you eaten some unpleasant substance and made yourself vomit? Have you caught an Earth virus? Is that it?'

'No, it isn't it!' Opal opened the shower doors a fraction, flung out her *Human Handybook* and slammed them shut again.

Uncle Bixbite flicked through the book. 'Very useful, I'm sure. But where is your Full and Final Earth Report? Come along, don't keep me waiting.'

Opal pushed the doors aside, fully this time. She stood up and threw back her cloak. 'I've something to tell you, Uncle Bixie. It's no good smacking round the shrubs any longer. I'm just going to come right out and say it.' Her eyes flashed nervously. 'The fact is, I haven't got a report. I'm completely empty-fingered.'

'Empty-fingered?' Uncle Bixbite looked appalled.

Martha swallowed. She knew she needed to speak up. It was now or never.

'Yes,' said Opal. 'I haven't got a report because . . . because—'

'Because I've got it,' Martha burst out before Opal could continue.

Everyone stared at her. Opal, Uncle Bixbite, Robbie, Garnet and Uncle Bixbite's mingle. Martha felt like running home there and then, but she held her ground. She had to.

'I've got Opal's final report.' She thought she'd said it quietly but her words seemed to ring out, as sharp and clear as bells.

'You?' said Uncle Bixbite in disbelief.

'No, you haven't, Martha,' Opal said. 'You can't

have the report because it doesn't exist.'

'Yes it does.' Martha took a deep breath and pulled the folded sheets from her pocket. 'It's here. I'd like to read it to you, Sir . . . Your Majesty,' she said to Uncle Bixbite, 'if that's all right with you.'

Opal snorted. 'It isn't all right with *me*,' she said. 'It's all *wrong* with me.'

But Uncle Bixbite put up his hand to silence her. He nodded to Martha.

It was her signal to begin. She opened out the sheets of paper. Her hands shook and she had to cough.

'I'm not surprised you've got a toad in your throat, Martha,' said Opal. 'You're making a big mistake here. I can tell.'

'Opal!' scolded Uncle Bixbite. 'Let the child speak. I, for one, am interested to hear what she has to say.'

Opal sat down in the shower again.

'Opal Moonbaby's Full and Final Earth Report,' read Martha. 'Prepared by Permanent Earth Dweller, Martha Stephens.'

Opal folded her arms across her chest. Martha tried not to notice; she just hoped that by the time she reached the end of what she had to say, Opal would understand.

'Opal Moonbaby has been on this planet for a year. That year has been the best year of my life. In that year I have got to know Opal very well. I think I know her better than anyone on Earth does, or anyone on Carnelia. In fact, I think I know Opal better than she knows herself.'

She looked up, half expecting Uncle Bixbite to tell her the report was pointless and irrelevant, to tell her to stop. But he was sitting down on the Minmangulator, arranging the flaps of his jacket.

'I once told Opal she would make a rubbish queen. Well, that's not true. She'll make a brilliant one. I know that, and these are the reasons why.'

Opal covered her ears with her hands and looked up at the shower head. She said, 'Yadder-yadder-yadder, blah-blah-blah!' But Martha had begun. She wasn't going to let Opal put her off now.

'Number One. Opal will introduce new foods such as popcorn and marshmallows so that Carnelians won't have to eat tasteless scoff capsules all the time.'

She nodded to Robbie, who knelt in front of Uncle Bixbite with the shoe box. He had been clutching it so hard it was starting to bend in the middle. He lifted the lid and handed Uncle Bixbite a packet of sweetcorn seeds and a bag of marshmallows.

Uncle Bixbite frowned, but he took the packets. Martha went on quickly.

'Number Two. Opal will make sure Carnelians have fun. Even the grown-up ones. She'll teach people the games she's learnt on Earth, and people will laugh more and be happier.'

Robbie brought out an old pack of Top Trumps and a box of dominoes and balanced them on Uncle

Bixbite's knees. When he added a travel set of Snakes and Ladders to the pile, Uncle Bixbite started as if he thought the snakes on the lid might jump up and bite him.

'Number Three,' Martha read. 'Opal will be kind to the mingles of Carnelia. She won't have them re-minmangulated after only a year. She'll have them refreshed instead, like Garnet has been, so that they can keep well and stay with their owners forever.'

Robbie handed Uncle Bixbite a feather. It wasn't as big as the one he had jammed the Minmangulator with, but it gave the general idea.

Chi-chigga-cheeeee! Garnet yelped excitedly. He leaped up and flew round the room. The terrapin mingle looked on, a little enviously, Martha thought. She stole a glance at Opal, who was sitting inside the shower cubicle with her cloak over her head, looking like a large purple flowerpot. Martha couldn't see her face so she didn't know how she was taking all this.

Martha's mouth was starting to feel dry now but she carried on, sending the next part of her speech in Opal's direction.

'Number Four. The main reason that Opal will be a brilliant Queen and Coronet-holder is that she is an amazing friend. She's funny, and she knows what you're thinking. She's loyal and she's brave. She'd climb up and down a mountain to save a friend, no matter how steep it was, and she always keeps her promises. She tries to, anyway. Even if it hurts her to do it. Even if it isn't the right thing for her.' Martha swallowed. Her voice was cracking a bit, but this was no time to start crying. 'Opal Moonbaby is the best friend you could ever have.'

Opal didn't make a sound, but Martha thought she saw her shoulders twitch. She hoped Opal wasn't furious with her, but even if she was, there was no going back now.

Uncle Bixbite touched the feather to his chin and Martha could tell he was paying close attention to what she was saying. It made her feel braver.

'Carnelia is a lucky, lucky place to have Opal Moonbaby. Every planet should have an Opal. Logic might not always be king when Opal Moonbaby is Queen, but that won't matter. Because Opal Moonbaby rocks! And when she rules over it, Carnelia is going to rock too. We'd love to keep Opal on Earth if we could, but we can't. Because Earth isn't where she belongs. It would be wrong to make her stay.'

She stopped reading and spoke directly to the Opal flowerpot. 'I won't do that to you, Opal. I won't let you do that to yourself. I won't let you be a homesick tiger.'

Opal popped her head out at last. She looked straight at Martha, and Martha looked straight back. She felt as if they hadn't looked at each other properly for days, not since the night Opal had left Stormhaven.

You know I'm right, Martha thought hard. I know you only said you'd stay because of me. But you mustn't, Opal. You've got so much to do on Carnelia. I'll miss you, but I'll be OK. You've been my best friend, but now you'll be the best friend of a whole planet. I think it's your fate, Opal, and I think you know it too. You've known it all along. It's written in the stars. I think it's been written there for a long time.

Martha felt exhausted. She had done it. She had nothing more to say, but she could tell from the way Opal's eyes were shining and deepening that her words were having a big effect.

Opal began to speak, but she was distracted by her hair, which was suddenly springing and sprouting out of her ponytail. Every strand of it popped up on the top of Opal's head again, and waved about there like lively octopus tentacles. The elastic band that had been holding the hair in place snapped and shot across the room, pinging into Uncle Bixbite's cheek.

Martha and Robbie gasped as his hand flew to his face.

But Opal laughed. 'That's what we Earth dwellers call a cow's eye, Uncle Bixie!' she hooted. 'A hole in once! How's that for good shooting!' She carried on chuckling, and Martha saw that her eyes had returned to their proper shade, the colour of violets in full bloom. 'Mind you,' said Opal, 'Martha did it, really. It was nothing to do with me.'

Opal smiled at her then, and Martha felt a huge wave of relief rush over her. It was a smile that proved Opal did understand, that she wasn't angry with her. It was a smile that showed Martha she really had done the right thing.

'You're not going to give us a lecture, now, are you?' she heard Robbie say, still kneeling in front of Uncle Bixbite. 'Not like the one you gave Opal on holiday?'

Uncle Bixbite looked perplexed. He studied Robbie, his eyebrows meeting in the middle in a curious V shape. Then he smiled at him, and laughed. Martha had never heard him laugh before. He laughed louder and louder, letting out great big breathy guffaws.

'Well, well,' said Uncle Bixbite when he could speak again. 'I see that you have learnt a great deal on Earth, Opal, after all. And I see that things will be different when you hold the Coronet. Far be it from me to stand in the way of progress. One thing is for sure, Carnelia has interesting times ahead.' He looked at the array of items on his knee. 'But this food, these games; they're all a mystery to me. You'll have to explain.'

'We'll start now,' said Opal. 'No time like the current. What shall we play? Hide and Seek, Snakes and Ladders or Blind Man in the Buff?'

'Blind Man's Buff!' said Robbie with a giggle.

'Good choice,' said Opal, and she pulled Uncle

Bixbite's handkerchief from his pocket and tied it around his eyes.

'This is a very simple game, Uncle Bixie. All you have to do,' she said, spinning him round, 'is find us.' She spun him a few more times and they all tiptoed away.

'No peeping!' Opal cried. Martha saw her filling up the scoff-capsule dispenser and switching it on.

A batch of warm popcorn shot into the air and rained down on Uncle Bixbite. 'Now!' Opal yelled. 'Scoff and sprint!' Everyone grabbed handfuls of the popcorn, stuffing it in their mouths, and then charged away from Uncle Bixbite. He ate some too, nodding approvingly behind his blindfold.

'Interesting effect on the taste buds,' he said. 'I think Carnelians will enjoy this.'

'Oh yes, they're in for a treaty!' said Opal from behind the Minmangulator. 'Now hurry up and chase us, Uncle, will you?'

Uncle Bixbite plodded about the room as Martha, Robbie and Opal, Garnet and even Uncle Bixbite's mingle, ran, sidestepped, dodged, flew and scuttled around, all steering clear of the King of Carnelia's outstretched arms.

Before long, the Domestipod was hot and sticky and full of munching sounds and laughter and very little oxygen. Eventually, Uncle Bixbite grew dizzy and toppled over Mrs Underedge's parachute silk, where it lay bundled up in the corner still waiting to be collected. As he fell, he caught Robbie's ankle and tackled him to the floor. At the same time Martha fell over Uncle Bixbite's feet, narrowly avoiding squashing his mingle. Opal, not wanting to be left out, threw herself on top of them all while Garnet flew down, landed neatly on her head and folded away his wings.

They lay there all together, rocking slightly, in one big, happy, sweaty, alien-mingle-human heap.

'Playing Twister? Can anyone join in?'

Sam was in the doorway with Mum, their arms linked.

'Sorry to disturb you, Bixbite,' said Mum, trying not to smile. 'I didn't realise you were so ... busy.'

Uncle Bixbite took off his blindfold. Deftly he dropped it on top of his mingle and tucked them both away in his breast pocket.

'Come in, come in,' he said. 'You're very welcome. We were just having a little leaving party.'

'Leaving party?' said Mum. 'Who's leaving?'

'I am,' said Uncle Bixbite. 'Along with my niece. We have been called away.'

As he spoke, Martha felt cool air come floating into the Domestipod and curl itself around her, reminding her of what was about to happen, of what she had made happen.

'Called away?' Mum said. 'Where to? Will you be going far?'

'Quite a few thousand miles,' Robbie answered.

'Oh, I get you,' said Sam. 'Being posted to NASA,

are you? Off to the USA? New space mission, I expect.'

'Something . . . along those lines,' said Uncle Bixbite.

'Say no more.' Sam tapped the side of his nose. 'I understand. Classified information. Your secret is safe with me.'

'When are you off?' asked Mum.

'We leave tonight.'

'Tonight?' Mum sounded shocked. 'Oh, no! We'll miss you, Opal. Very much.'

Martha's heart lurched. She had known exactly what she was doing. She had planned for this. She had wanted her plan to work, too. It was only now that it had, that it was beginning to sink in that she really would have to say goodbye to Opal forever. Her chest hurt at the thought. It was too soon. It was all happening too quickly. Uncle Bixbite was already starting to usher them all out, talking about making final preparations for their flight. What if she couldn't see Opal on her own again? What would she do then?

Opal took her hand. 'We'll say a proper goodbye, Martha,' she whispered. 'Wait by your window, tonight. Don't fall asleep. It might be very late when I go. Don't drop out, whatever you do.'

Martha smiled miserably. 'I won't drop off,' she said. 'I'll stay awake forever if I have to.'

It was incredibly painful having to wait for nightfall to see Opal again. Uncle Bixbite had insisted on spending time alone with her, giving her lectures about her Coronet-training and making sure she was ready for take-off. Martha and Robbie had stayed in the play area for the rest of the afternoon, rocking backwards and forwards on the swings, trying, and failing, to catch a glimpse of her through the Domestipod window.

Later, they had surprised Mum by getting into their pyjamas even earlier than she normally started asking them to. It was still only dusk when they stationed themselves by the window in their room. They were much too early, but they were so eager for the moment when they would see Opal again,

even if it was for the last time, they couldn't help it. They dragged Martha's desk and chair over. Martha sat on the chair and Robbie sat on the desk. He put Yoyo next to him on a squashy burst football, and the three of them faced the window and waited.

They sat for hours, but the Domestipod's door remained closed and there was no sign of Opal. Birds flitted across the front of her little house, stocking up on food before going to roost. Why was Opal taking so long?

Gradually the light faded and the traffic died down. Mum and Sam chatted in the kitchen. Every now and then one of them laughed. Evening dog-walkers came and went. Some of them hurried, checking their watches as if they needed to get back for the start of some TV programme. Others strolled about, taking their time, letting their dogs roam around the old copper beech tree, letting them sniff at every lamp post. It was odd to see people going about doing all their usual things, unaware that life as Martha knew it was about to change forever.

Night fell.

Still nothing happened.

Eventually Robbie's head started to loll. 'I'm not going to sleep,' he insisted, resting his cheek on Yoyo's football.

Martha kept watch as Robbie's eyes closed and his breathing became deeper. She heard Mum and Sam use the bathroom, then the click as the light went out in the hall, the closing of Mum's bedroom door.

An eerie silence settled over the Half Moon Estate. Martha felt rather than saw the clouds roll in. The few stars she could see seemed to flicker and grow dim. She stared harder at the Domestipod, sensing that something was about to happen.

In the darkness, the Domestipod began to glow. Gently at first, then more strongly until the whole house lit up, shiny pink and purple. A breeze blew on the flowers around it. They waved their petalled heads to and fro and then they began to lift into the air, along with the Domestipod.

'This is it,' Martha whispered. 'She's going.'

Robbie didn't stir.

She opened the windows wide and watched the Domestipod hover and then rise further. For one awful moment she was afraid Opal was going to go straight back to Carnelia without saying goodbye, but then the Domestipod slowly revolved until its window was facing Martha's window, and it moved forward, sailing gently over the play area and drawing level with their flat.

Opal was standing at her window too. She was wearing her travelling cape. Its collar stood up like a ruff around her throat. Her spiky hair shimmered round her head in the reflected light of the Domestipod, like a crown. Her eyes shone. She was very still. Seeing her like that, framed by the window, Martha remembered the very first time she had seen her, standing in the doorway of the ground-floor flat. 'About zooming time!' she had said then. 'I thought you were never zooming coming!' And Martha almost hadn't gone in. What she would have missed if she hadn't!

Opal blinked and her window slid open.

'Hello,' she said.

'Hello,' Martha replied. She felt almost shy.

'We've got this wrapped round our elbows,' commented Opal. 'We're not meant to be saying hello, are we?'

'Not really.' Martha smiled.

'We're meant to be saying goodbye, so longing and farewelling. But I need to say thank you, too.'

'Do you?'

'Oh, yes. You made a fine speech about me this afternoon, Martha. Uncle Bixbite was most impressed. And look what he gave me.'

Opal held up a white ribbon that hung around her neck. A medal dangled on the end of it. It wasn't gold or silver or bronze. It was a solid mass of glittering white gemstones, diamonds and pearls. Three letters stood out among them, picked out in purple stones. CIA.

'Your Carnelian Independence Award!' exclaimed Martha. 'You got it!'

'I never would have,' said Opal, 'if it hadn't been for you. Thank you for that, Martha. And thank you for making me see.'

'I didn't make you see. You can see better and further than anyone.'

'Oh yes, I can see for kilometres. I can see through walls and over oceans and up drainpipes, but I couldn't see what was right for me. For my future. You had to see that for me.'

Martha shrugged. She hadn't seen it at first, either. She had wanted Opal to stay so much.

'You wouldn't be truly happy on Earth, Opal. Not forever.' She smiled. 'And I know you'll make a great queen.'

There was a pause and then Opal blurted out, 'You wouldn't like to come with me, by any chances?'

'What? To Carnelia?'

'Yes. Why not? You could be my special advisor. You're such a wise young owl, Martha. You could help me with Matters of Planet. And the Coronet-holder should have a friend, a companion counsellor. I won't find a friend as good as you on Carnelia, you know. There's no one up there like you.'

Martha shook her head. She was amazed. It had never crossed her mind that it was even possible for humans to go to Carnelia.

'It's never been done before,' Opal admitted. 'There might be a few adjustments to make. Gravity-boosters, breathing apparatus, or some such. You might need to wear a special suit, I suppose, but I'm sure we could sort it.' She stuck out her bottom lip. 'We'd find a way.'

'That's a lovely offer.' Even though Opal hadn't thought it through properly, Martha knew she meant it. She knew too that she could never leave Robbie and Mum. Sam was probably moving in with them in a few days; she'd need to help sort things out in the flat. And there was Jessie. What would she do if Martha disappeared? She couldn't leave her on her own doing quadratic equations with Mrs Underedge all year. Besides, she wanted to go to school; there was so much stuff she wanted to learn. She would be going to secondary school next year. She was looking forward to wearing the new uniform. Opal knew what was in her future, but Martha wanted to find out what lay ahead for her too. Her future wouldn't be the same without Opal in it, but she realised now that she was looking forward to it all the same.

'You belong on Carnelia, Opal. You know you do. But I belong here. In Archwell.'

Opal nodded, but she seemed very sad.

'Imagine if I did come, though,' said Martha, to cheer her up. 'Imagine if I came right now! I'd love to see Uncle Bixbite's face when I stepped out of the Domestipod.'

'He'd burst a flood vessel!' Opal grinned. 'I wouldn't like to be in your slippers then.' She reached out of the window with both hands. Martha reached out too and their fingers met, making a bridge over the long dark chute of air below.

'You'll visit me one day, Martha,' Opal said. 'I know it.'

The Domestipod began to whir, powering up for the long journey ahead.

Every moment counted now. Martha felt the seconds ticking away like precious last heartbeats. She held Opal's hands and looked at her long spindly fingers with their knobbly knuckles. Perhaps she would never see those hands again. It was time to say the last things, the important things, the things that urgently needed to be said. But she couldn't think what they were.

'Send us a postcard,' she said suddenly. It sounded so silly. There was no plane or post van going between Opal's planet and hers. They couldn't send letters or emails or anything. Even the worldwide web couldn't reach as far as Carnelia. 'A postcard . . . or . . . a message in a bottle . . . or something.' She smiled and felt helpless.

'I'll stay in touch somehow,' said Opal. 'You'll see. We're star sisters now, remember. We can't ever really be parted, not completely.'

She clutched Martha's hands fiercely. Neither of them wanted to let the other go.

Garnet, who had been sitting quietly on Opal's shoulder, leaped out of the Domestipod and into the bedroom. He landed on Robbie's back and started licking his face.

'Hello, boy,' said Robbie, coming to. His cheek was

red from lying on the football, and it had the imprint of Yoyo's face in the middle. 'Hey!' he said when he saw what was going on. 'Why didn't you wake me? Is that your CIA, Opal? That's well extreme! I've got a leaving present for you, Garnet.'

He picked up an old cake tin and opened the lid a fraction. 'It's got bark chips from the play area, Earth leaves and cat biscuits.' Garnet sniffed at it appreciatively.

Robbie hesitated. Then he said, 'And I want you to have Yoyo.' He picked up the old, frayed monkey and held him out to the mingle. 'I don't really need him any more. And I think Yoyo will have fun on Carnelia.'

Martha knew how much Yoyo meant to Robbie. He'd had him since he was a baby. It must have been very hard to give him away. It proved just how much he loved Garnet, but she knew that already.

Garnet took the toy very gently in his mouth, taking care not to puncture it with his teeth. He couldn't make any sound, so he revolved his head as if to say thank you and farewell.

'Bye-bye, Garnie,' said Robbie. 'Have a nice life.'

'That was kind of you, Cucumber Hero,' said Opal. 'I have a little some-such for you too, actually.' She dug in her pocket and brought out two sparkling objects shaped like trophies. She passed them in through the window, one for Robbie and one for Martha.

'*Robbie Stephens*,' Robbie read. '*Carnelian Award for Ingenuity and Geniusness.*' He grinned. 'Storming! Who needs a world record when you've got one of these? What does yours say, Martha?'

Martha looked at her own shimmering trophy. Its silvery surface was engraved with spidery letters.

Martha Stephens
Secret-keeper, life-saver and friend
The best friend a Carnelian ever made

She couldn't read the words out loud because she was afraid of crying.

Opal spoke instead. 'I've had a fantabulous year with you, Martha. I've learnt so much from you. I'll never see or hear or think about a single zooming thing without imagining what you would see or hear or think about it first. I may not be with you in the skin and the teeth in future, but I'll definitely be with you in my spirits. And if you ever, ever need me, I'll be back. No matter how busy I am with Matters of Planet. If you're in trouble I'll shoot down to Earth like a javelin. I'll be with you like a shot-put!'

'That's so lovely,' Martha managed to say at last. She would remember those words always, and the trophy was beautiful. She really wanted to give Opal something in return but it hadn't occurred to her until now. She felt stupid for not thinking of it before. 'I'm sorry I haven't got anything for you, Opal. I wish I'd got you a souvenir.'

'Oh, oh, but you did,' said Opal, suddenly all excited. 'You have given me something, Martha. You've given me this!' She pointed to her eye. For a moment Martha didn't think there was anything different about it, but then she saw a fat, wet blob glistening in the corner. The blob spilt over and trickled down Opal's cheek.

'A real, genuine Earth tear!' breathed Opal. 'I never thought I'd be able to make my face leak like a human's. Not in a zillion years. But I did it! I did! I'm crying!'

She threw back her head. 'What a leaving present! I cried an actual Earth tear! Woohoo!' she told the dark sky.

She looked back at Martha. 'Hug me now,' she said. 'And then I'll go.'

'What?' said Martha. 'Now? Are you sure?'

'Hug me, Martha,' Opal said again.

Martha did. Keeping one foot on the floor, she leant out of the window as far as she dared and hugged Opal. She took a deep, deep breath, inhaling Opal's strange scent of sparklers and hot chilli peppers. She needed to remember it forever.

After a minute, Opal took her by the elbows and gently pushed her back into the safety of the bedroom. She held Martha's fingers in her own for one more moment. Then she let them go.

Robbie was hugging Garnet so hard he looked as if he was going to squeeze all the life out of him, the life they'd worked so hard to put back.

'The time has come, Cucumber Hero!' Opal cried, flinging her arms out wide. Robbie released Garnet at last and the mingle nuzzled his cheek one final time, then flew out of the bedroom window and onto Opal's head.

Opal opened her eyes very wide and then wider still.

As Martha and Robbie watched, her eyes grew as large and round as saucers. Their violet centres filled up with new shades of purple, turquoise, bright blue and green. More colours than Martha could count swam and danced around inside them. Their light filled the room. A light so strong and startling, it drove Robbie and Martha back towards the bunk beds, dazzling them with its brightness.

Opal lifted a hand. 'This is it, Earth dwellers. This is so long, fare you well and cocka-toodle-oo. It's not goodbye for all eternity, though. Because I'll see you again one of these nights. You'll see. And you'll see me, too.'

A cloud of smoky light gathered beneath the Domestipod and the whirring sound grew louder.

'Wait!' Martha wanted to shout. But she knew it was too late.

Opal swirled her eyes once and the Domestipod rocketed up into the sky.

Martha rushed to the window just in time to see a zigzag of purple lightning tear across the night.

She watched it lose its sharpness. She watched it fluffing outwards like an aeroplane trail, the drifting tail of a shooting star. She watched until it faded away completely. She watched until the sky was dark again.

Then she turned to Robbie.

'She's gone.'

'Gone,' he echoed.

There was nothing else to say. It was over.

Opal Moonbaby had left the Earth.

'**M**y treasure! Oh, my treasure!'

Martha woke from a dream in which she had just lost a big chest full of treasure. The sun was streaming into the room and it took her a few moments to realise that someone was shouting.

'I've lost my darling treasure!'

Whoever was outside could be heard very clearly through the open window. Martha and Robbie had left it wide open when they had finally gone to bed, perhaps in some slight hope that Opal would change her mind and come back in through it.

Martha sighed. This was it, the first day without Opal Moonbaby. She wasn't as depressed as she'd thought she would be; she even felt quite proud of herself, of the way she had helped Opal leave Earth.

But she wondered how long it would take to get used to waking up in a world without Opal in it.

'Oh, my treasure!'

Martha knew that voice. She got up and went over to the window. Mrs Underedge was hammering on the door of A Cut Above. She seemed to be wearing a nightie under her coat and her new trainers were muddy.

'Bonnie-Belle-Flower-Lady!' she wailed. 'She's gone!'

Mum came out of the salon and spoke to her in a gentle way, trying to calm her down.

'But I've been searching all morning,' Martha heard Mrs Underedge cry. 'I don't know where she could be!'

Martha shook Robbie. 'Wake up,' she said. 'We've got to help find Bonnie-Belle-Flower-Lady. She's lost.'

Robbie groaned. 'Did I really give Yoyo away?'

''Fraid so,' Martha said.

She ran out into the hall and straight into Sam.

'Hiya,' he said. 'I was just coming to see if you two were OK. You've been asleep half the morning.'

'Mrs Underedge has lost her dog,' Martha told him as she stuck her feet into her shoes.

'Uh-oh,' said Sam. 'I'll come and help look for her, shall I?'

'Thanks,' Martha smiled. She passed him his trainers. 'These stink, by the way.'

Sam put his nose to the shoes and pulled a face. 'Ew! You're right. They do.'

✶ ✶ ✶

Mum was doing her best, but Mrs Underedge wouldn't be consoled. She was pacing about on the pavement, wringing her hands in despair. 'Where can she be? Where can she be?'

'Have you checked the park?' Sam asked.

'I've scoured every inch of it. There's no sign of her.'

'We'll find her for you,' said Mum. 'Don't worry.'

'It's all right, everyone.' Robbie arrived. He had stuck his new trophy in the top of his pyjama trousers. 'We'll soon have this sorted. We just need a bit of Robbie Stephens Ingenuity and Geniusness. Now spread out and start searching.'

Martha was just wondering where to look for the best when Robbie said, 'What's that yellow stuff sticking out of the pipe?'

Martha knew what it was as soon as she saw it.

Mrs Underedge's parachute silk. It was stuffed inside the concrete play-pipe. Opal must have left it there.

The entrance to the pipe was almost entirely blocked by the yellow silk. Martha touched it tentatively. She would never be able to play parachute games at school again without thinking of Opal. Robbie took hold of it to pull it out, but Martha stopped him.

'Did you hear that?' she said.

'No. What?'

They kept still and listened.

'That,' said Martha. A muffled sound, a sort of squeaking, was coming from inside the pipe.

Martha and Robbie pressed down the parachute silk with their hands and peered in.

Bonnie-Belle-Flower-Lady was nestling in the cosy yellow bed, stretched out and sleepy. She seemed very contented. She wasn't the one making the squeaking sound.

There was another, tiny creature in the pipe with her, lying on Bonnie-Belle-Flower-Lady's side. It had a furry body and pointy ears. It had minute hairy paws and odd little nobbles, like tiny elbows, on its flanks. It was making a strange noise. If Martha had been asked to describe the noise, she would have said it was a cross between a puppy whining, a kitten mewing and a baby barn owl having its first go at hooting.

'You don't think . . .' she said slowly.

The creature opened its amber eyes as if to see who was speaking.

'That couldn't be . . .'

Martha held her breath as the creature turned its head. It turned its head all the way around, in a circle.

'. . . could it?'

'Yes,' said Robbie, grinning all over his face. 'It could. It definitely could!'

They reached into the pipe and stroked the tiny animal. 'Can I hold her?' Martha asked Bonnie-Belle-Flower-Lady. The little mother dog didn't stir as Martha gently lifted her baby out of the yellow nest. She was no bigger than Martha's hand. Martha gasped. She could feel herself falling in love with her already.

'How do you know it's a girl?' said Robbie.

'Don't know,' said Martha. 'I just do.'

'Garnet's baby!' Robbie said. He stroked the minuscule creature, his eyes round with wonder. 'Hello,' he kept saying. 'Hello. Hello.'

Chu-chu, said the creature, making them laugh.

'Do you think Opal can see this?' Robbie said. 'From Carnelia?'

'I'm not sure,' said Martha, 'but I think she knows about it.' She remembered the way Opal had stared at Bonnie-Belle-Flower-Lady's plump stomach when they had last seen her in the park.

By the road, Mrs Underedge moaned again and Martha remembered she still thought Bonnie-Belle-Flower-Lady was missing.

'Over here!' she called. 'It's all right. They're safe. We've found them!'

'Them?' said Mrs Underedge vaguely, as she and Mum hurried over.

Martha held out the creature for Mrs Underedge to see. The teacher leant heavily on the play-pipe. She looked as if she might faint.

'What on earth is that?'

'It's Bonnie-Belle-Flower-Lady's baby,' said Martha. 'Her . . . puppy, I mean. Isn't she gorgeous?'

'No!' Mrs Underedge looked appalled. 'This isn't right. Bonnie-Belle-Flower-Lady shouldn't be having puppies yet. And when she does, she should have five or six. And they shouldn't look like that.' She grimaced at the creature. 'What are those . . . those *protrusions* on its sides?'

Wing buds, Martha thought but didn't say. She was stunned to think that something half-Carnelian was still here on Earth with them.

'They're so peculiar,' Mrs Underedge went on. She touched her nose with her hanky. 'I wanted to mate Bonnie-Belle-Flower-Lady properly. She should have pedigree puppies, not mongrels like this one.'

'Aw, I think she's cute,' said Mum.

'Adorable,' agreed Sam, back from searching behind the flats. 'She's a little gem.' He stroked the tiny animal's head with one finger.

'I can't keep her.' Mrs Underedge blew her nose.

'Could *we* keep her?' Robbie looked eagerly at Mum. Martha knew she would say no. She had always said there wasn't room for a pet in their flat. Now that Sam was moving in, there would be even less.

'Well,' Mum said. She looked at Sam. 'Maybe.'

'Yes,' said Sam. 'It depends on you two, really.'

'On us?' Martha didn't understand.

'Yes, the thing is,' Mum said, 'our flat's too small for a pet. But . . .'

'Mine isn't,' finished Sam.

'Oh, yes,' said Robbie, ''cos you've got a garden.'

'So,' said Martha to Sam, not sure what they were getting at, 'you mean, *you*'d keep her?'

'No,' said Sam. 'I mean, *you*'d keep her. I mean, *we*'d keep her. She could live in my flat. And so could you. We could all live there together.'

'I've been trying to talk to you about this all week,' Mum said. 'Only I've been so busy at the salon and you were so busy being with Opal. You see, Sam's suggested that rather than him moving in with us, we all move to his flat instead.'

'It's not much bigger than your place really,' Sam said. 'But it does have an extra room.'

'Yes,' said Mum. 'Sam's cleared out his back room for you, Martha, if you want it. If we move in with him, you and Robbie can have a small room each.'

'No more burst footballs to get in your way,' added Sam.

'And it's on the Half Moon Estate. It's only round the corner,' Mum went on. 'So you'd still be able to come to the play area, go to the mini-market, see Jessie, do all your usual things.'

'But only if it's what *you* want,' said Sam, looking at her seriously. 'We'll only go ahead with the plan if

257

you say yes, Martha. It's your decision. We'll only do it if you and Robbie say yes.'

'I say yes,' said Robbie immediately. 'I say it's a no-brainer. A garden to play football, my own room and a new pet too. What's not to like?'

'Martha?' said Mum quietly.

'What d'ya reckon?' said Sam. They waited for her to speak.

'I don't know.' Martha stroked the little animal in her hand. It felt warm, and its wet nose nuzzled into her fingers. 'What do you think, Gem?'

Gem. Sam had said it first. It was just the right name. It suited the little creature perfectly.

Gem sat up on her soft little hind legs and said *chu-chu-whee*. Then she walked about on Martha's palm and scratched at it as if it was garden soil. She rolled on her back, displaying her tummy which was white with tiny orange spots and stripes.

Martha looked up. Sam and Mum were holding hands. She thought how right they looked together, but they were watching her anxiously. They could have just decided what to do and told Martha and Robbie that was how things were going to be from now on, but they hadn't done that. Mum was happy with Sam, but she really wanted Robbie and her to be happy as well. Sam wanted them to be happy, too. She could see that now. She and Robbie were going to have new rooms and a garden and a pet. But, most importantly, they were going to carry on living their lives in Archwell with Mum. And now with Sam, too. She couldn't think of anything on earth that would make her happier.

'Yes,' she said. 'I'd love that, Sam. Let's do it. I think that would be fantastic. I think it would be . . . extreme!'

Star Sister

A crisp and clear October evening is one of the best times to see the stars. How many there are! How they glitter and gleam, like patterns of sequins pressed into the night.

On this particular night, one of the stars breaks free from the others and zigzags away, rushing downward, towards Earth. It comes quickly and surely. The tiny star seems to know where it is heading. Which country, which city, even which estate.

It homes in on its target, circling a block of flats, hurdling over an old copper beech tree, flicking round a corner. It slows down at last. Barely more than a spark now, but a lively one, it flies through a garden and hovers outside the window of a ground-floor flat. It's just an ordinary flat the star has settled on, but it has found what it has been seeking.

The curtains are open and the scene inside is clearly visible. There's a family birthday party going on. A boy sets a big cake down on the table. Eleven candles stick out of the icing, shimmering and shining. A dark-haired girl sits in front of the cake while the people gathered around her, a woman, a man, the boy and another girl, about her own age, sing her a loud and cheery Happy Birthday song.

Outside the star sizzles and – it can't resist this – turns a somersault.

An odd little animal sitting on the birthday girl's shoulder pricks up its ears and flashes amber eyes at the window. It makes a piping sound like yapping or hooting. The girl reaches up to calm it.

'Hush, Gem,' she soothes. But then something makes her look towards the window too.

The star seems to fizz in the air. It changes colour. White turns to silver, then violet, then back to white again. It dances through colours as if it is dancing a special dance especially for this girl.

The girl smiles slowly, a smile of wonder and perhaps recognition. 'Star sister?' she whispers.

Her attention is drawn back to the table for a moment as the man says, 'Three cheers for Martha!'

'Hip, hip, hooray!' the party cries, loud and cheerful and loving. 'Hip, hip, hooray! Hip, hip, hooray!'

'Right,' says the man, rubbing his hands together. 'Let's get some games going!'

The girl smiles and glances back at the window, but it's too late. The star has already gone. Up to the sky, shooting back to its rightful place in the galaxy.

The star has gone, and it has taken a piece of the girl's heart with it. The girl isn't sad about this. She is happy. She knows the star will keep that piece of her heart with it always.

It will look after it, too.

And it will remember her. Just as she will remember.

Forever.

Martha's decided friends are stupid.
She never wants another one. Ever.

So when Opal Moonbaby comes along, with her mad silver hair and huge violet eyes, claiming to be an alien and wanting to be friends, Martha is definitely NOT interested. But Opal isn't the kind of alien who takes no for an answer...

Sparkling with originality and charm, this is a heart-warming, hilarious story about friendship.

978 1 4440 0478 6

£6.99

Opal Moonbaby is an alien. She reads minds, has a special brain dictionary, which is a bit muddled, and a pet who is a mix of six different animals. She's also Martha's best friend.

Martha can't wait to take her to school – but she has no idea what will happen when they get there!

A laugh-out-loud funny, heart-warming and original story about friendship – and aliens!

978 1 4440 0479 3

£6.99